The Ugly One

The Ugly One

The Childhood Memoirs of

Hermione, Countess of Ranfurly

1913–39

MICHAEL JOSEPH

LONDON

MICHAEL JOSEPH

Published by the Penguin Group
Penguin Books Ltd, 27 Wrights Lane, London w8 5tz, England
Penguin Putnam Inc., 375 Hudson Street, New York, New York 10014, USA
Penguin Books Australia Ltd, Ringwood, Victoria, Australia
Penguin Books Canada Ltd, 10 Alcorn Avenue, Toronto, Ontario, Canada m4v 3b2
Penguin Books (NZ) Ltd, Private Bag 102902, NSMC, Auckland, New Zealand

Penguin Books Ltd, Registered Offices: Harmondsworth, Middlesex, England

First published 1998
10 9 8 7 6 5 4 3

Set in 13/18 pt Monotype Perpetua
Phototypeset by Intype London Ltd
Printed in Great Britain by The Bath Press

A CIP catalogue record for this book is available from the British Library

ISBN 0-718-14333-7

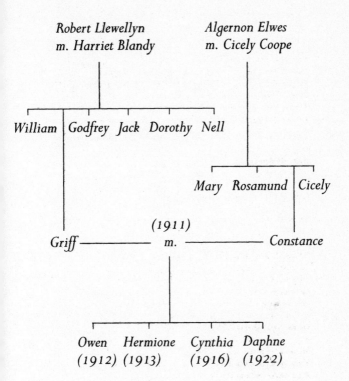

Family Tree

Prologue

I started life as a disappointment – because I wasn't a boy. I continued being a disappointment – because I was ugly. My older brother was handsome; my younger sister was beautiful; and my little sister was our baby and people always say babies are beautiful even when they are hideous.

After a while I got used to being told I was ugly and gave up minding about it. Instead of minding, I determined to ride better, run faster, be funnier and give more generous presents than the rest of my family. But underneath these efforts I never forgot for a moment that I was ugly.

At school, mercifully, there were even plainer children than me. These generally were more amusing than the beautiful ones.

But new problems kept arising – bosoms and bottoms, for instance. I was luckier than most and didn't have much of either but I felt sorry for some of my contemporaries who, even when quite young, became weighed down by abundance of both. Often, far into the nights, we discussed what could be done about these weighty problems. Of course bosoms and bottoms could be cut off and fed secretly to our dogs but how about the mess and grown-up fury about the laundry bills? And what if our dogs did not like bosoms and bottoms?

My sister and I found growing up difficult. Parents continued to treat us as children and so did staff. Horrors, like 'monthly periods', descended upon us. Ghastly 'suitable friends' and 'suitable clothes' were provided for us. Swiftly we learned how to destroy the clothes – on one wonderful morning Nannie Kate fished six ruined outfits out of a lavatory – but the young friends who were invited to lunch, tea and supper were more difficult to shed. Though we pinched, kicked and sometimes bit them they arrived regularly in frilly clothes, with fastidious manners and futile conversations. Our parson's daughters were the worst: they said 'Pardon' every two minutes, were afraid of dogs, and wore gloves to eat tea.

It was easy to like animals and birds and a few grown-ups, though many of our elders used ridiculous voices to talk to children. When we went upstairs to bed, we mimicked them to amuse Nannie Kate. Our mother never changed her voice for anything or anyone. She had a beautiful voice even when she was angry. She was very pretty and gentle and could bewitch people, animals and birds. Robins used to come into her bedroom and watch her getting dressed.

We were a very happy family: our father and mother were divine to us, and so was

Nannie Kate. We had comfy beds, good food and wonderful animals to take care of. Love and laughter surrounded us until, quite suddenly, this stopped. To our horror and dismay our parents divorced. Overnight our happiness vanished.

The Llewellyn Family

My Welsh grandfather was born in 1848 and his name was Robert William Llewellyn. He inherited two estates in South Wales: Cwrt Colman near Cardiff, and Baglan, halfway between Briton Ferry and Aberavon. He died before I was born.

The early history and myths of this part of Wales go back deep into the dark ages and are now so interwoven it is difficult to disentangle one from the other. On the two properties were huge boulders, large round barrows, ruins of small castles, fortified camps and watch-towers but few could be identified or dated accurately and, though tales were legion, truth remained a will-o'-the-wisp. In 1697 a Welsh antiquary referred to a grave at Baglan, 30 feet long with stones at each end, which was said to be the grave of Dilic the Giant. But who and what and when was Dilic?

Facts began to emerge in the eleventh century when, despite the Norman Conquest, the Welsh lords of Afan ruled the area between the rivers Neath and Avon, where Baglan lies. From then on Aberavon became the hatchery of local rebellion against the Normans and the English. From the mountains and the valleys, by stealth, came the sure-footed, freedom-loving Welsh to pounce upon, harry and destroy those who dared invade or occupy their lands. With devastating fury, they lashed out and then vanished again to their hidden strongholds. Nearly always the owners of Baglan and their tenants were at the forefront of these raids, which continued throughout the Middle Ages.

By the fifteenth century the highway through Baglan, along which pilgrims journeyed to St David's Cathedral and the shrine at Penrhys in the Rhondda, became also the path of poets and revolutionaries. Baglan then was a haven for bards who had mastered the intricacies of Welsh metres and their songs link us vividly with local history and scenery and describe Owen Glyndwr's rebellion and Owen Tudor's imprisonment and execution at Hereford.

Since about 1250 a little coal had been worked in Glamorganshire and in the sixteenth century monks owned pits at Margam, halfway between Baglan and Cwrt Colman. From then on the mineral wealth of South Wales was gradually to change the landscape and the way of life in the mountains and the valleys.

In the eighteenth century a Boulton and

Watt steam engine had been installed at Baglan colliery and iron mines existed in the parish. Now barges moved in and out of the havens and creeks along the beautiful coast where once smuggling had been a sport. And, as more and more veins of this black wealth – coal – were discovered, quarrels began between old friends – landowners and workers – and accidents occurred in the pits. From time to time these ignited into riots. Copper smelting and silver refining warmed up tempers too: the Industrial Revolution brought back to Wales some of the fury and frustration of medieval times.

The Llewellyns who owned Baglan and Cwrt Colman also held land in Pentre, Aberavon and the Rhondda Valley. They claimed to be descended from Morgan Vychan, Lord of Afan and Afan Wallia, who died in 1288. One of these, Griffith Llewellyn II, who was born at Brombil House in 1804, was a shrewd businessman who was interested in the history and literature of Wales. He had influence and wealth and made an impact on the affairs of Glamorganshire, where he was a JP, High Sheriff and keen churchman. He owned a pottery and brickworks at Baglan besides being closely connected with the collieries in the Rhondda, where he established with others the firm of Llewellyn and Cubitt, engineers, iron and brass founders.

It seems as if Griffith Llewellyn II and his wife were determined to pay back some of their good fortune to Glamorganshire and the list of their endeavours is long: they added a new wing to Swansea Hospital; built St Peter's Church at Pentre and St Catherine's at Baglan; they improved Baglan School and built a house for the headmistress; they built almshouses for the old in Neath; restored St Mary's Church in Aberavon and other churches in Swansea, Neath and London, and contributed to St

Catherine's in Melincrythan. They maintained
a missionary in India and created the 9th
Glamorgan Rifles. Griffith had properties in
Baglan, Aberavon, Melincrythan, Hirwaun,
Pentre, Boedringallt, Ynsfaio, Penrhys Isaf and
Cwmdare. In those days it must have been an
exhausting job to take care of these estates so
widely spread and to watch over his business
and charitable projects as well, but somehow
he crossed the mountains, marshes and
moorland on horseback and still found time
to go to church with the utmost regularity.
He died in 1888, childless, and the properties
came, via his first cousin, to Robert Llewellyn,
my grandfather.

Grandfather Robert Llewellyn married
Harriet Blandy of Kingston Bagpuize, who
bore him four sons and two daughters. Her
family was always referred to as 'The Black
Blandys' – perhaps because they had settled in
Madeira and built up a good business there.

Robert sent his eldest son, William, to Eton;
the next two, Griffith and Jack, to Winchester,
and his youngest son, Godfrey, to Dartmouth
Naval College. His daughters, Dorothy and
Nell, were educated at home. Griff, his second
son, the wildest and gayest of them all, was
his favourite and my father.

From his childhood, Griff seemed to possess
some extra energy or electricity which caused
him both to be forever in a drama and quite
fascinating to other people. At five he fell out
of the family carriage and was severely
concussed. At six he was thought to be dead:
after shutting him in the nursery for being
naughty, his Nannie returned at dusk to let
him out and found the window open and a
huddle of clothes on the lawn below. Later he
was found naked, squeezed underneath the
nursery chest of drawers. At Winchester he
was nicknamed 'The Goat' because of his
endless adventures and pranks. At New College,

Oxford, he went shooting, hunting and dancing: he drove the New College and Magdalen coach, wrote poems and played with motor cars: no one could understand how he managed to pass his exams.

One dark summer night in 1906, soon after he came down from Oxford, Griff went with his brothers and farm-hands to help put out a fire on Aberavon mountain and, as they stood in the smoke beating out the flames, he stepped backwards over the edge of a 40-foot quarry. He was carried home on a hurdle and lay for months unable to move: the doctors said he might never walk again and anyhow must wear a steel corset for the rest of his life. Whenever he was alone he rolled off his bed and crawled round the floor: it was very painful but gradually he managed to move about on all fours. Months passed and he began to stagger about on his legs. And then one day, to the astonishment of all the family, he came galloping up the drive on his favourite pony, which he had caught and saddled. Soon he was dancing again, driving to balls in his Delahaye car or his two-seater Naggant. In 1908, when he was thought to be fit enough to work, he joined a firm in London which sent him first to Ceylon, tea planting and, later, to Burma, rubber planting.

In 1910 Robert Llewellyn died and Griff returned home. Perhaps my grandfather thought his favourite son would never fully recover from his fall and be able to fend for himself – anyway he left Cwrt Colman and its land to his eldest son Will and the Baglan estate to Griff. My grandmother would live at Baglan Hall for the rest of her life and my father in any one of the pleasant houses on the estate which he would own and run. My uncles Jack and Godfrey were left only £1,000 each and it is typical of them both that they never referred to this without laughter. My Aunt Nell married but Aunt Dorothy donned a long blue veil and decided to give her life to the Church. My grandfather was buried in St Catherine's churchyard at Baglan and my grandmother, heartbroken, wore black until she died.

The Elwes Family

My English grandfather was born in 1855 and his name was Algernon Elwes. He was the second son of John Henry Elwes and Mary, daughter of Sir Robert Bromley of Stoke Park, Newark. The Bromleys were descended from Ruperta, the daughter of Prince Rupert the Cavalier and his mistress, Mrs Hughes, an actress.

The Elwes family lived at Colesborne, halfway between Cirencester and Cheltenham in Gloucestershire. They were descended from Sir Gervase Elwes, Lieutenant of the Tower

of London in the reign of James I, who was
hanged at Tyburn after being accused of
poisoning Sir Robert Overbury, a prisoner in
the Tower. The slow, frightful and mysterious
death of the thirty-two-year-old poet
Overbury, in 1613, remains an unsolved
murder but it seems certain some terrible bond
of secrecy existed between him, the Earl of
Somerset and the King himself, who may have
planned the crime and its 'cover up'.

The family house at Colesborne in the
Cotswold hills was small though the lands
were considerable, and in 1852 it was pulled
down and a much larger and uglier house built
in its place. During this upheaval Algernon and
his elder brother, Henry, were taken by their
father on his schooner yacht, the *Fairy*, for a
long cruise round the Mediterranean. Apart
from this their early journeys were mostly to
Congham in Norfolk, the home of their uncle,
Robert Elwes, who wrote *A Sketcher's Journey*

Round the World. Both six feet two inches tall
with massive frames, Algernon and Henry were
singularly handsome, but their lives were to
be very different.

Algernon loved English country life and was
happy, shooting and fishing and staying at
home with his family or visiting friends.

From his prep-school days Henry had a
passion for watching birds and later he became
equally enthralled by trees, plants, butterflies
and insects. He went to Eton and then joined
the Scots Guards but neither deterred him from
his obsession with nature. From the age of
seventeen he never spent an unbroken year at
home: his love of travel, sport and natural
history took him away incessantly to explore
his own and other people's countries. In 1865
he went to the Hebrides and soon afterwards
to Greece and Turkey. In 1870 he toured
India and went to Madras, Calcutta, Darjeeling
and Sikkim. In 1874 he sailed to the Greek

islands and revisited Asia Minor. He returned
to India and Nepal in 1876, 1879 and 1880
and, in 1886, he explored the route known as
the Rishi-la to Tibet and made a trip to the
Singalela Range during the rains and another
to the Khasi Hills. In 1888 he set off for North
America and Mexico. He spent most of 1891
in Belgium, Brittany and in Norway, where
he researched elk, bear and reindeer. He went
often to the Alps to collect mountain plants.
In 1895 he returned to North America, this
time to see Canada. In 1898 he made a great
journey across Central Asia and Siberia. He
travelled to South America in 1901–2 and
crossed the Andes from the Argentine on mule-
back to explore Chile. In 1911 he went to the
Malay Peninsula, Java and Formosa. He
returned once more to Nepal in 1913–14.

By boat, train, paddle steamer, sailing ship
and canoe; by carriage, wagon or on foot;
often mounted on horse or mule, this gentle

giant explored deeply and carefully into the
countries he visited, making copious and
accurate notes. Sometimes he learned to talk
to his guides and bearers in their own languages;
always he was generous over his discoveries.
He returned home with remarkable collections
of trees, plants, birds, butterflies and insects
and his beneficiaries were the arboretums,
private properties and museums of England,
and Kew Gardens. In spite of his huge stature,
loud resonant voice, his exactitude and hungry
impatience to learn, he got along well with
great and humble people and never forgot
those who had helped him enjoy and discover
their country. Maybe he is still remembered
in legend along the tracks and trails of other
lands where his enthusiasm, energy and
remarkable appearance might not easily be
forgotten. In England he became President of
the British Ornithological Union, the
Entomological Society and the Royal English

Arboricultural Society. He was the author, with Professor A. Henry, of *The Trees of Great Britain and Ireland*, a book which is still unchallenged on its subject.

When at last he grew old, he stayed at home with his patient wife, Margie, to watch over his estates and supervise his garden, which contained astonishing varieties of orchids, lilies and rare plants. Then he wrote to a friend: 'I have during my life taken an active part in most outdoor sports and occupations. I have crossed and re-crossed the Himalayas and the Andes, explored Siberia and Formosa, shot and fished in Norway and, as I grow older, I find there is more companionship, consolation and true pleasure in gardening and in plants than in anything I have tried.'

When Algernon Elwes, my grandfather, left Eton he went into business. He married Cicely, daughter of Octavius Edward Coope, and lived at Bibury Court in Gloucestershire until he moved to Nottinghamshire to join his father-in-law's firm.

Octavius Coope, whose grandfather had been one of the founders of the London Hospital in 1756 and whose father had helped create the Phoenix Assurance Company in 1782, also excelled in business: with his friend Ind he built up the brewing firm of Ind Coope in 1830. He was short, tubby and always wore a wig. He married a beautiful wife, who adored him, and was Member of Parliament for Great Yarmouth for many years and later for Middlesex and Brentford in turn. He was a keen supporter of the Church and fox hunting, and a collector of pictures and china. Above all he was compulsively generous: one day, on hearing the London Hospital was short of funds, he immediately sent an anonymous donation of £10,000; on another he met an acquaintance who was in trouble and lent him £4,000. He built a church in Whitechapel and supported it, leaving his business flourishing and his six children and their families exceedingly well off. He left £1,000 to each of his grandchildren and a request that one of them, Charles Ponsonby, should eventually become a Governor of the London Hospital though, at that time, Charles was only seven years old.

Periodically Algernon Elwes visited South Africa in connection with Cape Breweries but mainly he lived and worked for Ind Coope in Nottinghamshire. He had four daughters, Mary, Constance (my mother), Cicely and Rosamund. Whenever he had time to spare, he took his wife and children hunting, shooting or fishing. He loved home life, was a great reader and storyteller and was devoted to his own and the Coope families.

Soon after Octavius Coope's death – just when Algernon's three eldest daughters were grown up – trouble began. Octavius' only son was obstinate and had no business ability and the Managing Director of the breweries was rash: neither would take advice nor listen to the warnings of members of the Board or family. Around 1904, through bad management, Ind Coope went bust and slid into the hands of receivers. This was a catastrophe for the whole Coope family, whose money was invested in the firm: suddenly my Elwes grandparents, the Ponsonbys of Woodstock, the Guise family in Gloucestershire, and the Ruggles Brise family of Spains Hall in Essex were almost destitute. Octavius' fine collections of pictures and antiques were auctioned at Christie's; my grandfather sold his house and most of his possessions and moved into a small house on the edge of London; the other families stayed in their large houses but in dire straits.

Not long after this, Algernon became crippled by arthritis and could no longer work regularly: now he rode a tricycle instead of a horse and moved about the house on crutches. My grandmother struggled to help him; kind friends invited the eldest girls to visit and go hunting and dancing; Rosamund was sent to a boarding school at Malvern. On Christmas Day 1937, he died.

1910, 1911, 1912

By the end of August 1910 Griff Llewellyn grew restless. After the death of his father he stayed near his mother at Baglan through the spring and summer and kept himself busy with the Guernsey herd, a new pig farm and the harvest. Suddenly he longed to get away. He contacted his brother Jack, who was studying for an exam at Cwrt Colman, and suggested they should go and spend a weekend with their Winchester College friends, Frank and David Mitchell, who lived at Highgrove near Tetbury in Gloucestershire. Griff drove his Delahaye along the coast and across the hills to Cwrt Colman and then the two brothers left the mountains and small fields of Wales behind, crossed the River Severn and climbed the steep road up into the Cotswold hills.

The following day the Mitchells took Griff and Jack to lunch with their uncle Henry Elwes at Colesborne, where their cousins Mary, Constance and Cicely Elwes were staying. During lunch, and afterwards in the big library which was filled with almost as many rare flowers as books, Griff could not take his eyes off Constance: she was beautiful, tall and graceful, with dark brown hair, large blue eyes and a tiny nose. When it was time to leave and the brothers climbed back into their car, Griff told Jack he would marry her come what may.

From that day on, wherever Constance went Griff and the Delahaye followed: if she took a train he would be at the station; if she went to a ball he would contrive to be invited; if she visited friends he would get a room at a nearby pub and wait about, if only for a glimpse of her; and if she stayed at home, he called incessantly.

At first Algernon Elwes was surprised and dubious about this dark, good-looking, obstinate young man, but gradually he grew to like him. The pursuit, which continued throughout the autumn and winter, ended at the altar of St George's Church, Hanover Square in London, in April 1911.

After their honeymoon Griff and Constance went to live in a pretty house on the Baglan estate. They were supremely happy: together they wandered the seashore and explored the miles of marshland, where snipe, woodcock and wild duck abounded; or they would stroll up through the gardens and meadows past whitewashed cottages and farmhouses, to spend all day alone in the mountains. Only when they set out to visit friends or family was there a cloud in their sky. Baglan was beautiful but it was an oasis flanked by rapidly growing industrial areas: to the west lay Neath and Swansea; to the east sprawled Aberavon and Port Talbot. For all the mountain and farm land he owned, Griff felt hemmed in: chimney stacks, slag heaps, factories and rows of bleak little houses seemed to be forever creeping closer and now only the curves of the nearest mountains hid them from view. The highway through Baglan was no longer a path for pilgrims and poets: it had become the main road to miles of metal monsters which encircled the coast of South Wales with a strength and permanence no Norman or English invader had ever achieved.

In February 1912 their first child was born, a dark-haired son they named Owen. Soon afterwards Griff determined to move away: his

mother who, for so long, had watched over
the parish, the Church, the families of workers
and tenants, and the gardens, was happy at
Baglan Hall and had enough time and money
to carry on. He would help her run the farms
from a distance but not stay to watch the slow
but sure invasion of industry over the land he
loved. He talked this over with his mother and
Constance and happily they agreed. When
spring came, Griff set out to search for
somewhere else to live.

1912, 1913

High in the Cotswold hills, above
Winchcombe, which used to be a royal town
– the home of Mercian kings – is a great house
called Postlip. It is a lonely place: in the
distance it seems to be wedged in a fold of
the hills and surrounded by trees but from the

Postlip Hall, 1912

Owen and me at the seaside in Wales, 1914

(*above*) Owen, Mummy and Rosinante, our Shetland pony who arrived by car, 1914

(*left*) Owen, Mummy and me, 1914

(*opposite top*) Daddy with his two chargers, Tactful and Gray, the Dell, Aylsham, 1914

(*opposite bottom*) Mummy and Daddy dressed in each other's clothes for a fancy-dress party!

Aged two, 1915

(*above*) Owen and I loved each other very much

(*below*) Owen and me playing with the 'Noisy Horse', 1916

Daddy saying goodbye to Owen and me just before sailing to Egypt, 1916

windows of its three wings there are long and peaceful views. Above the house is a small twelfth-century chapel from which flights of wide stone steps lead down through terraced gardens to the drive, where two great stone dragons guard the entrance to the house and the way to the stables below.

In 1912 Griff discovered this house empty and fell in love with it. He tried to buy it but the old Roman Catholic lady who owned it would not sell to a Protestant. Finally, after weeks of argument, he persuaded her to lease it to him. On 12 October he and Constance moved in with Owen, their greyhounds, Hermes and Juno, and a cheerful and adequate staff. They also brought their horses and Pilgrim, the groom from Baglan, and the nursery cat and goldfish.

All through that winter Griff and Constance went hunting and shooting and family and friends came to stay. They furnished the house extravagantly with antique furniture and it became as pretty and comfortable inside as it was elegant outside. It seems they learned quite soon that the house had a curious history – but no one seemed to care. In the evenings, when they sat around the big log fire in the panelled hall, they got used to the dogs suddenly leaping up – as if they were marionettes all pulled by one string – to race up the polished staircase to the first and then the second floor, bristling and barking at something no one ever saw. Venus, a middle-aged and portly bulldog who came to stay with Aunt Cicely Elwes, insisted on staying at the foot of the stairs all day and night: she would lie there, waiting and watching until, quite suddenly and for no apparent reason, she would growl ferociously and hurtle up to the attics, where she snarled, scratched and slobbered at the walls until Griff went to carry her downstairs. Then she would resume her

vigil in the hall and, sooner or later, hurl herself
upstairs again.

Spring and summer came and Postlip looked
more lovely than ever. Griff rode in point-to-
points, coursed greyhounds over the wild,
shaggy hills, and began to transform the
garden. Constance was expecting her second
child and stayed at home, playing with Owen
and stitching her tapestry. The family Visitors
Book filled up with more and more signatures,
and photographs of friends and animals.

On 13 November 1913, I was born in the
west wing of Postlip and they named me
Hermione. Whatever shared Postlip with us
became more disturbing: the monthly nurse
who came for my birth seemed undaunted
when her apron strings were pulled undone
whenever she went to the powder closet in my
mother's bedroom or carried me along the
passages to show me to visitors in the upstairs
drawing room. She told my mother there was

much talk in the servants' hall about footsteps in the night and the strange death of a young maid which had occurred before we took over the house. 'I am not afraid of ghosts,' she said, 'but I do hope this house is not cursed.'

Christmas came and our grandparents, aunts and uncles arrived to stay, as well as a tall, attractive young man called Kenneth Gibson, who was engaged to my mother's elder sister, Mary. He was crazy about horses, racing and cricket.

In the early spring of 1914 it seemed as if life at Postlip would go on for ever: Owen rocked me in the oak cradle in the big hall and ruffled my dark curly hair; horses and dogs sniffed my pram as I slept every morning outside the front door, and there was happy laughter in the house, garden and stables. But in May, quite suddenly, we left and returned to Baglan. Was this because of talk of war, or something sinister to do with Postlip? I never knew.

1914

By June we were comfortably settled in Baglan Cottage, a fair-sized house halfway between Baglan Hall and the church our grandfather built. What conversations must have gone on around Owen and me in those summer days as catastrophe approached, but Owen was happy and busy picking celandines, buttercups and dandelions for our mother and making daisy chains to put on my fat wrists, and I was contentedly crawling about the lawns and carpets of our new home.

Our mother wore long, pretty dresses which swirled and swished when she moved. She played with Owen and me for hours on end: sometimes we went with her to the seashore and then I had to wear a sun-bonnet; or she would drive us in the pony trap to have tea with Old Margaret who lived in the Lower Lodge and always wore a shawl and a Welsh top hat. Often we went to the farm where Tuckey, our cowman, showed us the Guernsey calves, who licked our arms and legs, and afterwards we would ride on the hay wagons behind the great shire horses. When Rosamund, our mother's youngest sister, came to stay, we were put in panniers on Tom the carpenter's old cob and taken for picnics in the mountains; on the way down we paddled in the ice-cold water of the cwm.

Every Sunday we lunched with Gran Llewellyn at the Hall, where Lizzie kept the nurseries exactly as they had been when our father was a child. Lizzie had been a nursery maid then but now she organized Gran's hair and household and arranged the flowers – she was shy, tiny, and everybody loved her. Owen and I loved Baglan and its staff, many of whom had been there when our father was a boy.

Wherever our father and mother went they took us too, as if time itself might steal us from them. One wonderful evening we brought home a Shetland pony in the back of the car; it was four months older than me. My father gave it to Owen and my mother named it Rosinante. The next morning we were brought down early from the nursery: our father was standing in the hall dressed in a tunic with gold buttons, riding breeches and tall, shiny brown boots. He hugged and kissed us and our mother – and then he drove away. It was August, 1914.

We learned afterwards that our father and many of his friends had gone with their horses to camp on the racecourse at Hereford where the South Wales Mounted Brigade assembled. Our father belonged to the Glamorganshire Yeomanry and our Uncle Godfrey to the Montgomeryshire Yeomanry. In December the Brigade moved to Norfolk and made their

headquarters at Blickling Hall, near Aylsham:
this house belonged to Lord Lothian and was
surrounded by 400 acres of deer park and 5,000
acres of farmland, which made it an ideal place
to train cavalry. In our old Visitors Book there
is a water-colour sketch of a troop of the
Mounted Brigade standing at their horses' heads
with their backs to the Norfolk coast, while
helmeted and moustachioed Huns clamber up
the cliffs on ladders, and below is written:

Put your steelwork in oil

We're up in the morning before day is dawning
    To make ourselves soldiers we toil
We spend our time rubbin' our saddles with dubbin
    And putting our steelwork in oil.

We've no time to trifle with cartridge and rifle
    And no figure targets to spoil
For we're learning to fight, as is proper and right,
    By putting our steelwork in oil.

Though the foe sends his hosts to Norfolkshire
    coasts
  He'll never set foot on our soil
For we Yeomen will stand, an invincible band,
    Now we've put all our steelwork in oil.

1915

Just in time for Christmas 1914 our father
rented a small house called the Dell at Aylsham
for our mother, Owen, me and the dogs. We
stayed there until the autumn of 1915, when
the Brigade sailed for Egypt. It was wonderful
to see our horses, Tommy and Tactful, again
and they seemed to remember us and so did
many of the soldiers who came from Baglan.
'Indeed to goodness,' they said to us, 'you are
grown into giants.' Every day we rode a hired
donkey and on special days we went sailing on
the Norfolk Broads.

Owen and I spent much of our time with
the soldiers, who were always full of jokes
and kindness. When they groomed their horses
or cleaned their harnesses, they sang –
sometimes in Welsh, sometimes in English –
and when we were tired, they carried us home
to our mother and stayed for tea.

One night our Mother gave a fancy dress
party: some of the women wore their
husbands' uniforms and most of the men
their wives' dresses and hats. It was a specially
gay evening but Owen and I, who watched the
arrivals through the banisters halfway up
the stairs, did not understand it was a farewell
party till the next morning when the soldiers
and their horses went away. Owen and I kissed
all the men in our father's troop and waved
till they were out of sight. Then our father said
goodbye to us. It was dreadful – we'd never
before seen our mother cry.

A few weeks later, on our mother's birthday,

a beautiful 18–20 Siddley Deasy limousine
arrived. Tied to the steering-wheel was a little
note: 'Con. Many Happy Returns and ALL
my love. Griff.'

1916, 1917, 1918

When we returned to Baglan Cottage, early in
1916, we found that Gran had turned the Hall
into a hospital. Our Nannie took us there often
to see the soldiers. 'Hullo, baby, how's
Nurse?' they used to say, and laugh. Most of
them came from Australia and New Zealand
and all of them had been wounded in France.
Owen kept asking who had hurt them and
they always said, 'The bloody Boche.' Each
week ambulances brought more bandaged
soldiers to Baglan. On some days our mother
cried when she read the newspapers.

In October my sister Cynthia was born: she

had blue eyes and fair, curly hair. That winter it snowed and Owen and I had new overcoats and gaiters which buttoned up to our knees.

What a terrible year 1917 was. Not long after Christmas, Grandpa Elwes came to tell us that Aunt Rosamund had died of pneumonia at her boarding school in Malvern. She was sixteen. Grandpa looked crumpled and old. He told us that Grannie could not come to see us because she was ill with grief.

In April an artist, called Catherine Mayer, came to paint a portrait of Owen: he sat absolutely still in his best green velvet tunic and shorts, holding a bunch of celandines. Nannie told me I was too ugly to be painted.

During that year more and more of our friends left Baglan to go to the war: pretty Mrs Forty took over the cows from old Tuckey when he went to 'join up'; now girls looked after the cart horses and worked on the farm.

It helped that we had a baby in the house and that Juno was going to have puppies; and it helped that visitors still came to stay, though, except for Grandpa, they were all women and more and more of them wore black, like Gran. No one seemed gay any more except Tom the carpenter, who winked and made faces at us every Sunday in church when we sat with Gran and our mother in the front pew. Tom sang in the choir. Each morning and evening we said prayers with our mother: we prayed for our father, uncles and 'friends at the Front', for our dogs, horses, cows and Rosinante, and 'for those in sorrow, sickness or distress'. We also prayed for ourselves – that we be kind, good and brave. Right at the end we always prayed for 'the bloody Boche'. 'May God forgive them,' our mother said each time, but not lovingly.

Sometimes, in our house, grown-ups talked French, or stopped talking at all, when Owen and I were around. One day, when Cook was having her afternoon rest, Owen and I looked at her newspaper on the kitchen table: we saw dreadful pictures of men in mud; men in barbed wire; and men without arms or legs. And there were pictures of men all huddled together sleeping. Owen was five and owned a tricycle and he explained it all to me: 'There's been a quarrel between the Kings and Emperors,' he said, 'and now all the good men are fighting all the bad men.' He told me the sleeping men in Cook's newspaper were dead but they were heroes and would go to heaven.

In July Aunt Mary came to stay with her daughter Diana, whom we did not like. Juno our greyhound did not like her either and bit her in the face.

In August and September we returned to Postlip, which had been lent to our mother for eight weeks. Owen and I were frightened of that house and so were our dogs. At night our bedroom door kept opening though the latch was good. No one came in or spoke to us and each time Owen bravely shut it, but it always opened again. I used to climb into Owen's bed. We slept holding hands. Something or somebody lived at Postlip: who, or what, we did not know.

Soon after we returned to Baglan Cottage from Postlip, Owen became ill. He was taken to the Hall and put in the old night nursery, where my mother and Lizzie took turns to nurse him; he had pleurisy and pneumonia, like Aunt Rosamund. Every day, and sometimes in the night, Dr Phillips came from Port Talbot to see him. I was only occasionally allowed to go and peep at him from the door: he had a chamber pot by his bed and in it was thick yellow spit. Now I went alone to church with Gran on Sundays and Old Tom the carpenter did not wink any more, but he used to walk halfway home with Gran and me and sometimes I rode on his shoulders. He told Gran that when the spring came again Owen would be picking celandines and primroses 'same as ever'. Owen liked yellow flowers best of all.

As the weeks passed, I grew lonely; my mother was always with Owen, and Nannie took care of Cynthia. My sister was very beautiful, like a story-book child. She was our mother's favourite but Owen and I did not mind. In character she was quite different to us: she cried whenever anything was difficult or she wanted something and she clung to our mother wherever she went. She was an artist with tears and sulks. I spent my time with Hermes and Juno and every day I gave sugar lumps to Rosinante. In December an important doctor came from London to see Owen – his name was Lord Dawson. Afterwards I heard Nannie talking to Cook.

'It'll be a miracle if he lives,' she said, 'he is so weak and quiet now. We should never have gone back to Postlip – there is more in that house than meets the eye.'

At Christmas Santa Claus filled my stocking and my mother gave me a doll's pram. I was very excited because I was allowed to go to Gran's party for the wounded soldiers at the Hall, but when I got there they were singing 'Roses of Picardy' and 'It's a Long, Long Way to Tipperary' and for some reason or other I began to cry. Lizzie saw and took me upstairs. We tiptoed into Owen's room: he was breathing like Grandpa always did when he fell asleep in his armchair after Sunday lunch, in a kind of strangled snore. 'Talk to him,' Lizzie whispered, and for once she sounded fierce. I told Owen that Rosinante was all right, and that Juno's puppies were quite big, and I lied and said our father was coming home soon. Owen did not move or answer but, on the way downstairs, Lizzie said, 'Well done', and I felt better.

When the New Year, 1918, came, no one pretended any more: Nannie said Owen's life was hanging by a thread and I lived in terror that he would go to sleep for ever like the heroes in Cook's newspaper. I told Rosinante and the dogs. In church the vicar said special prayers for Owen and our family, and Old Tom in the choir cried and wiped his nose on his surplice. Dr Phillips came more and more often. My mother looked nearly as old as Gran.

Snowdrops and aconites began to come out in our garden and I counted them every morning. Now Cynthia could walk quite well but I had to guard her from Juno's puppies, which had grown strong and rough. Rosinante was losing her winter coat and we put little heaps of it on the lawn to help the birds build their nests.

In February, soon after his sixth birthday, Owen began to stir: he and the spring were coming back again – just as Old Tom had promised. After a while, when he was able to sit up in bed, I was allowed to watch him blowing coloured liquids through glass tubes from one big goblet to another. 'This is to strengthen his lungs,' Lizzie said.

At last Owen came downstairs for the first time. His clothes looked too big for him. The soldiers crowded by the front door of the Hall, even the ones on crutches, and they clapped and cheered as we drove off to Baglan Cottage in Gran's big car. It was marvellous to have Owen and my mother home again. I brought Rosinante and all the dogs into the drawing room to welcome them. Cook gave up playing our piano and Nannie stopped trying on my mother's clothes in her bedroom.

For a little while, our mother would hardly let Owen out of her sight, but gradually he grew stronger and we could all play together. One day, when the daffodils were tall, our mother set out in her pony cart to meet a visitor from London at Port Talbot station. They came back and had tea with us in the nursery. The visitor looked cosy and kind and rather like Gran: she wore a velour hat and a long black coat with a fur collar. She allowed Owen and me to stroke her big fur muff. Her name was Mrs Pankhurst. She had come to address a mass meeting in Briton Ferry. Next day Gran came to see us and was rather rude to our mother. She thought Mrs Pankhurst wanted to start a revolution and was a traitor.

All through the summer, ambulances continued to crunch up and down the gravel drive at the Hall and still our father did not return. A new Nannie came to look after us: she had ginger hair, a long nose and smelt awful on hot days. A governess, called Miss Williams, came every morning on a bicycle to

teach Owen, me and Cynthia to read and
write. She also taught us history and geography
in rhymes:

Long legged Italy kicked little Sicily
    Right into the Mediterranean Sea.
Austria got Hungary and ate up Turkey–
    And then there only remained Greece.

She was nice but, like all other grown-ups, she
would never talk to us about the war.

When the telegram arrived, we were with
our mother picking lavender in the garden.
Nannie brought it from the house: she held the
envelope out by one corner as if it was a
firework which might explode. Our mother
opened it carefully and slowly: we all watched
and saw that her hands were shaking. She
seemed to take ages to read such a little bit of
paper.

And then she stooped down and scooped all
three of us into a bundle and cried, 'Your

father is coming back. He's coming home soon. He'll be here soon, soon, soon . . .' We ran all the way to the Hall to tell Gran and she and our mother hugged each other and cried.

1918

Owen, Cynthia and I stayed by the front door nearly all day: we plaited Rosinante's mane, brushed the dogs and polished the tricycle and doll's pram. Inside our house, Cook was making a special dinner and Nannie was helping our mother deck the rooms with flowers. Around teatime we were dressed in our best clothes.

By the time our father arrived, we were quite tired and when he jumped out of the car we all felt shy of this wonderful hero. He had dark hair and a moustache; he was bronzed by the sun and his big brown eyes glittered with

laughter; he smoked a pipe and walked so fast
I had to run to keep up. He talked in a quick,
excited way. For the first time in our lives we
were allowed to stay up for dinner: Cynthia
sat next to him because he had never seen her
before.

For a whole week we did no lessons. Instead
we went, with our father and mother, all over
the farms and to every house and cottage. We
went round Gran's hospital and our father
talked with each soldier; we went up the cwm
to the mountains, and down across the
sandhills to the sea. We drove to Cwrt Colman
to see Uncle Will and Aunt Dolly – and we
tried not to look at her goitre. Our cousins
Robert, David and Francis were there and
their Nannie in her beaded bonnet. On the way
home we stopped in Port Talbot so our father
could thank Dr Phillips for saving Owen's life.
We spent a day by the sea, at Porthcawl, and
clambered over the rocks and paddled in the

pools. While we were having a picnic lunch we saw an aeroplane for the first time – it was flying in the sky. In church that Sunday Tom the carpenter sang so loud and joyfully that even Gran looked surprised.

Our father had come from the Middle East. At first he'd stayed with his Yeomanry and then he was made ADC to General Miller. Later he became a captain in Intelligence. He told us about Egypt, the Suez Canal and the battles for Gaza and Beersheba, and how, when Owen was lying at death's door, General Allenby had captured Jerusalem and driven back the Turks. He described the desert, the rocky hills and goat tracks of Palestine, the Camel Corps and the cavalry regiments from Australia, New Zealand and England. He had been to see where Jesus was born and where he died. He told us, sadly, that he had had to leave Tommy and Tactful behind. 'Thousands of beautiful horses have been left in Palestine,' he said, 'and God alone knows what will become of them.' Owen and I were spellbound by our Father and his stories, but we felt sad and worried about Tommy and Tactful.

On 11 November 1918, two days before my fifth birthday, the war ended. We lit a great bonfire at Baglan Cottage and Lizzie and Old Tom and hundreds of people came to see it. Up on the mountains and along the coast we could see other bonfires burning. People danced and sang. 'There'll never be another war,' they said. 'This was the war to end all wars – nobody died in vain.' Some of the wounded soldiers came in Gran's car but most of them were too ill to move or celebrate. Gran told us it would be ages before they could go home to Australia or New Zealand and added, 'The lucky ones, I mean.'

It was three years since we had been together for Christmas and my father insisted that all

Baglan should share in our happiness: Christmas trees were cut and decorated and every grown-up and child got a present; the wounded soldiers at the Hall were asked to hang up their army socks and Santa Claus filled them all. On New Year's Eve Owen and I were allowed to stay up late and we sang 'Auld Lang Syne'. 'Amongst other things,' our father said, as he kissed us goodnight, 'you are going to have a new Nannie in 1919: a Nannie who laughs and runs and loves the dogs, and who doesn't smell bad when it's hot.'

1919

A month later Nannie Kate arrived from Burton-on-Trent and, before she had even entered our house, Owen challenged her to race him across the lawn. She set down her suitcase, picked up her long skirt and ran.

Though she laughed all the way and her bun
of hair tumbled down, she won. She was not
tall or pretty, but her smiling face glowed
with kindness. We liked her at once and so did
the dogs and Lizzie. That first night, with two
white linen buttons and some Indian ink, she
made new eyes for Lily, my golliwog, who
had been blind for a long time. Next morning
she turned the big nursery cupboard into a
house for us; we called it Primrose Cottage
and furnished it with our miniature table and
chairs. We used our doll's tea set for parties
and made grown-ups knock before they
came in.

If it had not been for the two rabbits which
Tom the carpenter gave Owen on his seventh
birthday in February, we might never have
really understood the Depression which
followed the war. One morning our rabbits
disappeared from their hutch in the lavender
garden and Huw, our local policeman, came

to investigate. He found the rabbits in Aberavon – in a stew pot – and returned with their skins for us to identify. After a talk our mother went with Huw in her pony cart to see the thief. She took food and some of our clothes with her. When she returned she told us the thief was a young man with a wife, three children, no job and no money. She explained that, because of unemployment, hundreds of families were destitute . . . 'Things are getting worse every day in Wales and England,' she said, 'but it is far more terrible in Germany.' Cynthia began to cry but none of us knew whether this was for the rabbits, the thief, or the 'bloody Boche', and so our mother read us a story. On weekdays, after tea, she read fairy stories from beautiful big books illustrated by Mr Dulac and Mr Rackham; on Sundays she read Bible stories and our favourite was 'Joseph and His Many Coloured Coat'. That evening we made a plan to help the children of Aberavon, Port Talbot and Briton Ferry: our father promised milk from the Guernseys, bacon from the pig farm, and firewood; our mother would have sewing and knitting bees and deliver children's clothes in the pony cart. We'd give most of our clothes and toys, but not Lily my golliwog. Our bantams would give eggs. By bedtime, Nannie Kate had already started making gloves from our rabbit skins for one of the thief's children.

In the summer our mother and father went away often, searching for a house to buy. Baglan seemed empty and silent without them: 'The Moon and the Sun have gone out,' Owen used to say. But Nannie Kate kept us happy and busy: we went to see Mr Poole, Gran's head gardener, cleaning out the big pond at the Hall. He pulled lots of eels out of the mud and then, when they were dead, laid them on the lawn in a pattern so that they spelt

'Llewellyn'. 'You can eat only one, the rest must go to the hungry,' Nannie Kate told him. We visited the girls in the laundry and the boys in the bothy, and explored Gran's garages, which were full of horse carriages, pony and goat carts. We stole peaches, nectarines and grapes from the walled kitchen garden: 'For the poor people of Briton Ferry,' said Nannie Kate, though she ate quite a few. We called on Old Margaret, who taught us a little Welsh and allowed us to try on her top hat. Sometimes we went to tea with Mrs Poole at the Upper Lodge where a monkey-puzzle tree was growing. If her son, Dai, came home from the mines in time, we watched him have his bath in a tin tub in front of the fire and turn from black to white. We spent wet afternoons with Lizzie in the old nurseries, where we played with our father's toys and looked at his story books. Along the passage, in Aunt Dorothy's bedroom, was an altar and seven crucifixes. We seldom saw her because she went to church so often or was out helping the poor.

In the autumn of 1919, I was bridesmaid to our cousin, Diana Guise, in Gloucestershire. My mother and I went to stay for one night at Postlip, which had been bought by Will and Clara Muir, whose son, Kim, was a page at the wedding. In church Kim and I were wretched: we were dressed from neck to ankle in prickly gold brocade which itched and scratched our skin. When the register was being signed we were allowed to sit in a pew, where Kim wriggled until he wore out the seat of his trousers. Afterwards, as we walked down the aisle together holding the bride's veil, I saw his bare and very pink behind. At the reception which followed, Kim revenged himself by peeing on the back of the dresses of two elderly aunts and his Nannie.

After my mother had changed for dinner

and kissed me goodnight in the small bedroom next to hers, I listened to her footsteps pattering down the polished staircase to the hall – and then I remembered. That night I was sick all over a beautiful new eiderdown. Next morning a doctor was fetched. For six weeks I was too ill to be moved. The Muirs were very kind to my mother and me. They gave me a lovely doll on my sixth birthday when I sat up for the first time. Every night I listened to their dogs chasing something up the stairs, past my bedroom, and on up to the attics . . .

1920

Soon after we returned home, early in 1920, our father told us he had bought a place in Gloucestershire called Combend. Secretly Owen and I felt sad. All Baglan seemed to us to be a huge garden: the track to the mountains was lined with laburnum trees and the path to the church with daffodils; in spring the meadows were yellow with cowslips and buttercups; and there were carpets of bluebells, violets and primroses in the woods. Inside the great clumps of rhododendrons on Gran's lawns we made 'houses' where we climbed and played for hours. Hundreds of rooks lived in the tall trees along the drive and we loved them: Dai told us they called him for work in the mornings and welcomed him home each evening. 'Of course we'll come back for visits,' Owen said, when we went to farewell teas with Old Tom, Old Margaret, the Pooles and Lizzie. 'But it won't ever be quite the same: we won't really belong – we'll just be visitors.' We asked Huw, our policeman, to say goodbye to our thief.

Because our father was having major alterations made at Combend, we moved from

Baglan to Leckhampton Court, just outside
Cheltenham, which was lent to us by Aunt
Muriel Elwes for a year. Nannie Kate took us
by train with the luggage. We had fun on the
platform at Gloucester putting pennies into a
money box strapped to the back of an old
Airedale dog which collected for charity and
barked whenever a coin dropped into his box.
While we were doing this, a woman came up
to Nannie Kate, who was carrying my life-
sized Japanese doll, and said sharply, 'Madam,
are you aware you are carrying your baby
upside down?' We all howled with laughter
and she stumped off in a rage, saying she would
fetch the police.

Although Leckhampton Court had a large
garden and paddocks, we suddenly became
town instead of country children: no longer
were we allowed to roam or ride alone –
'because we do not know the neighbours'.
Hoops, tops and skipping ropes were

produced but we swiftly scorned them as 'pavement toys'. Nannie Kate loved to take us into Cheltenham, where we were bored while she investigated every shop. Each morning a new 'hat and gloves' governess arrived to give us lessons. Nannie Kate resented her and, behind her back, referred to her as Miss Hoity-Toity.

Once a week we were scrubbed and dressed in party clothes and bronze kid slippers to go to dancing class. We thought our teacher ludicrous and mimicked her when we got home: 'Nowh Girrls and Boyes. Point your toes and when the musick starts we'll go: "Uph, Downh, Rhound and Downh."' We were taken to a dentist who made a plate with a wire band to straighten my front teeth and gave Owen gas before he pulled out a tooth. We were measured by a tailor for riding breeches, tweed jackets and bowler hats. Our father gave us riding lessons and made little

fences for our ponies to jump. 'Remember,'
he told us:

'Your head and your heart keep up;
   Your hands and your feet keep down;
Your knees keep close to your ponies'
   sides –
   And your elbows to your own.'

Every evening, in the drawing room, our
mother still read us stories. Always beautiful,
with a magic voice, she kept us enthralled, and
when Nannie Kate came to collect us for
nursery supper, we clamoured for 'Just one
more story.' Later, when we had bathed and
put on our bed clothes, we'd leap on to the
nursery table and do skits on our various
teachers and household staff and would not
stop till Nannie Kate's big bun of hair had
fallen down from laughing. We knew that Cook
disliked our butler, that our gardener hated
dogs and children who spoilt his flower beds,

and that our chauffeur despised our groom
and called him 'Sitonyourarse'.

Nannie Kate made most of our clothes —
knitted jerseys, knee-high socks and caps with
bobbles on top. Overcoats and underclothes
were bought and the latter caused a riot every
Sunday morning when clean tummy bands and
combinations were issued. Owen and I had
quite a routine: while he threw tummy bands
on to the fire or out of the windows, I slit the
arms and legs of the combinations to turn them
into vests. Cynthia, who was delicate and
better behaved than us, never joined in. We
all adored and spoilt her. She was very pretty,
short and frail and as blonde as Owen and I
were dark. Mummy absolutely treasured her
but we did not mind that she was the favourite.
She had a white rabbit fur coat to wear on
cold days and she always managed to get one
or other of us to lace up her shoes or boots.
We all loved her but she had a different life to

Owen and me – we had to bung along and she never did.

Before long we were taken to see Combend. It was ten miles from Cheltenham, Gloucester and Cirencester and two miles from Elkstone village. A mile-long lane off Ermine Street, the Roman road, led to it and its 5,000 acres. We found an old farmhouse and a big barn covered with scaffolding, and a chapel, stables and sheds all being altered. Most of the windows had 'eye-brows', and all of it was built in stone. Electricity, central heating, panelling, oak floors and telephone were being installed. Our father was also laying out gardens and improving the stables. A lovely pond below the house was full of trout. Combend was nearly as remote as Postlip and, except for a few scattered cottages, no other house existed for miles. High on the hills the wind fairly whipped across the land and some trees leant permanently as if they were afraid

of it. We thought it wonderful, but Nannie
Kate said it reminded her of Wuthering Heights
which, Owen told me, must be the place
where she worked before she came to us.

When Christmas came again, I stayed awake
because I wanted to thank Santa Claus for
coming and I'd got some sugar lumps under
my pillow for his reindeer. I was astounded
when our mother and father arrived with a
torch and began to fill my stocking. Later,
when we were opening our parcels around the
Christmas tree, I noticed that Aunt Dorothy
had sent all three of us religious books and,
unfortunately, I remarked, 'If Father
Christmas is a lie perhaps Jesus is too.' The
silence which followed was only broken by
the sound of Nannie Kate's hairpins dropping
to the floor. As I watched her hair collapse
and her shoulders shake I listened to the
punishment I was going to get. For a long time
afterwards Owen and I puzzled about Jesus: if

he was just another story, why had Arthur Rackham and Edmund Dulac done no pictures of him; if it was true he could do miracles, why did he not save himself?

After Christmas we returned, with Nannie Kate, for a short visit to Baglan to see Gran. At Port Talbot station, where Gran's car met us, there were hundreds of men standing about. 'What are they waiting for?' asked Owen. Gran's chauffeur replied, 'For work and wages. Mostly they are miners who are having a dreadful time.' We found Gran's house was no longer a hospital. She took us to see all our cousins: we raced up the mountains and down across the sandhills to the sea; we told her about Combend and that our mother was expecting a baby. We had a lovely time.

Since we were very young we had known and loved the miners. We admired them tremendously for the dangerous work they did. Always smiling and singing – sometimes in

English, sometimes in Welsh – many of them were the sons of our family's employees. We'd played football with some of them on Gran's big lawn when we were small. They were wonderfully gentle and friendly. Once when I was ten, some of them took Owen and me down a mine. This was strictly forbidden, which made it all the more exciting. At first I felt rather afraid of going but after a ride in one of the little trucks I thoroughly enjoyed myself and only worried how I should explain my dirty clothes to Nannie Kate.

1920, 1921

Because Leckhampton Court was rather a gloomy place, our mother took us out often. We went to see Uncle Ken Gibson win the Amateur Riders' Steeplechase on Free Gift at Cheltenham Races and Owen won sixpence

from a bookmaker. Soon afterwards we went
to the wedding of our favourite uncle, Godfrey
Llewellyn, who married Dossie Kennaird: she
wore a long hideous dress and train over
Bluebeard-type diaphanous trousers. We
went often to see Grandpa and Grannie Elwes
who lived in a house with a walled garden
close by the gates of Cirencester Park, where
Grandpa gave us rides on the back of his green
tricycle. The park gatekeepers, who wore frock
coats and top hats, always saluted Grandpa as
we pedalled by – perhaps because he was a
Justice of the Peace.

We loved our grandparents, though Grannie
was apt to give us little 'good talks'. However,
we disliked her 'companion', Miss Rowe. With
gloom-and-doom talk, she managed to
interrupt all conversations, and she was vile
to the staff. She was marvellously unattractive:
big bottom, big bosom, big nostrils and a
moustache. Her thin falsetto laugh and her

condescending voice, together with her ludicrous clothes, made it difficult not to mock her. She always wore mauve knitted outfits with hats to match and carried a mauve handbag which contained mauve-framed spectacles and a mauve silk purse. She used three different voices to speak to the staff, Grannie and us children. When she had a birthday, Owen and I gave her some mauve lavatory paper. Our cook said she could not make a mauve birthday cake for her, so a sandwich cake appeared decorated with rather nasty sugar violets.

Grandpa couldn't bear her and referred to her as 'that woman', but Grannie, who was as near to being a saint as you can get, hauled us all up for a lecture. 'Just imagine how you'd like to wake up in the morning with a face and figure like poor Miss Rowe, with your parents dead, very few friends and almost no money? And, having got a job with a kind family like ours, think how you'd feel if the grandchildren mocked you and sniggered at your conversation and every movement you made. Apart from being rude, I think you are very cruel.' Then she pretended to cry a little, which she always did when she wanted to convince us that we were disgraceful.

One sultry afternoon when Miss Rowe went to sleep in a deck chair in the garden, Owen poured a tin of warm golden syrup over her head, body and feet. Her shrieks brought everyone running from the house and then there was a terrible silence: I saw Cook's shoulders shaking and I heard Nannie Kate's hairpins dropping on the lawn but we all watched Grandpa. For a moment I thought he was going to laugh but then he stiffened up like a turkey-cock and said, 'Outrageous' over and over again – and we were sent home in disgrace.

In those days it was the custom to call on

new neighbours. Our mother would put on tidy clothes and, of course, a hat. If the new neighbours were out, she would leave calling cards giving her name and address. The neighbours were expected to return the call, also in hats and tidy clothes.

For a while our mother took us with her on these excursions but soon she gave this up because these visits were so ridiculous and funny that we wrecked them with laughter. Mostly we did not like new neighbours who were more correct and lady-like than us. They thought we were barbarians because we scorned tidy clothes, tea-parties, hats and gloves. To be a fast runner, a swift swimmer or an ace climber of trees were our sinews of friendship. Above all, our love of animals eclipsed everything else.

One day an aunt asked why my sister and I were more loving and kind to animals than we were to our aunts and cousins. 'That is easy to answer,' I replied. 'You see, animals love and trust us and nothing ever deters them. Aunts and cousins are not faithful: they wobble and change their attitudes constantly, and always want to teach us something or other.' With difficulty I refrained from saying that animals are usually more attractive-looking than aunts – and often cleaner.

In one house we visited in Cirencester, there was a beautiful doll's house filled with miniature antique furniture. I liked best its little grandfather clock, which I stole. Nannie Kate found it later in the toe of my sock and there was a dreadful rumpus. 'Filthy little thief,' she said and sent me to bed without supper. Next morning I was made to return it to its owner. I was petrified as I stood on the doorstep after Nannie Kate had rung the bell. When I handed it back and apologized to the owner, he said, 'Please keep it always so as to remember me.'

Our first visit to our cousins at Colesborne was unforgettable: Great Uncle Henry and Great Aunt Margie were waiting for us in the library. She was a tiny woman who looked like a bird of prey, until she laughed; he was a smiling, handsome, bearded giant. He whisked Owen and me away to go round his garden and we saw Alpine plants; great hot-houses filled with orchids, lilies and tropical flowers; banks, borders and pond gardens ablaze with colour; and beautiful shrubs and trees. Afterwards he took us all over his house: a stuffed elk, a wild boar and a Burmese gong stood in the hall. Up and down stairs the wide passages were lined with glass cases filled with hundreds of large and tiny stuffed birds, and butterflies and insects of every shape and hue. It took hours to see them all. Uncle Henry talked to us as if we were important and answered all our questions, and he told us stories about the people and places he had visited. When we left, he gave us each a present: mine was a small leather-bound atlas. 'Learn it well,' he said, 'and one day go out and see the wonderful world.' He gave Owen a thin old book about John Meggot Elwes, who had died in 1763. 'He was an outstanding rider, a friend of Voltaire, and an incredible miser – one of our more eccentric forebears,' he said.

Uncle Henry's son, Cecil, kept a pack of foxhounds in their park. He was large, noisy and cheerful. He had been wounded in the war and had scars on his forehead and one of his eyes looked glassy. He'd been a colonel in the Scots Guards and won a DSO, and MC. We loved him because he was surprising: he flew a fox's brush from the radiator cap of his car and blew his hunting horn whenever he wanted to pass another car on the road. He was distinctly like the colonels in Bateman's amusing book. His quiet wife, Aunt Muriel, owned Leckhampton Court. They had one son and three daughters who were unusually tall and handsome and were a bit older than us. We loved them all.

Sometimes we went to stay with Sir Francis and Lady Price at Hensol Castle in Wales. On a lake in the grounds was a small island on which was a miniature replica castle, where we played for hours. Lady Price was a New Zealander and a superb rider. She thought nothing of jumping wire fences, much to our astonishment.

We had five great-aunts whom we liked to visit at Ledbury, Prestbury and Colesborne. Aunt Ethel had a squeaky voice and constantly made us laugh – she was awfully nice. No wonder she never married: she had such an appalling voice. Then there were Aunt Maud, Aunt Lena, Aunt Edie and Aunt Ros, who were all rather eccentric but most amusing. They wore black velvet ribbons to keep

up their double chins and they smelt of
lavender. I wrote a nursery rhyme about
them:

Buttoned boots, hypnotic hats,
    Parasols and Persian cats,
Lavender bags, cameo pins,
    Antique dolls and tiger skins;

Lace and frills on underwear,
    Chins and upper lips with hair,
Bosoms which all sport a rose –
    Awful drips on every nose;

Ruby rings on little hands,
    Tortoise combs, and velvet bands
Holding up their double chins –
    Royal portraits on their tins.

Lena, Ros, Edie and Maud
    Never, ever, make us bored,

And, we hope, that only death'll
    Part us from our dear Aunt Ethel.

How they must have longed to marry
    Some nice Tom, Dick or Harry –
But spinsters they'll be for ever –
    Though they're fun and very clever.

I left out Aunt Mitchell, who lived at
Highgrove, near Tetbury. She was
wonderfully good looking but she snubbed
everyone within reach and was beastly to staff
and dogs. Our mother called her the Ice Queen.
Also there was Aunt Helen, who had retired
to bed as soon as she grew up and had remained
there ever since. We kept a list of her ailments
which grew longer and longer. None of them
really existed – she just longed for pity and
presents. Our mother tried hard to be kind to
the aunts. Dressed in our best clothes and
sworn to behave well, we were taken to visit

them quite often. We dreaded these visits and occasionally rebelled. But one or two aunts we really loved and admired. We took them little presents of wild flowers, grass snakes and mice.

Uncle Cecil Elwes's hounds met at Combend before we moved in, and Owen, Cynthia and I went hunting together for the first time in our new breeches, jackets and bowler hats. We rode three Shetland ponies – Mousie, Midget and Rosinante. At the meet Mousie, who I rode, suddenly put her head down, let off a volley of rude noises and charged into the pack of hounds kicking and biting right, left and centre. Uncle Cecil turned purple and beat her off with his riding crop and shouted swear words at me. When the hounds moved away, I fell off three times in the first field, perhaps from delayed astonishment.

We all went to Great Uncle Henry Elwes's

Golden Wedding party at Colesborne. We
decided that he was special and that we would
give him some proper presents for his golden
anniversary. The cheapest cigarettes in those
days were called Gold Flake so we bought him
ten Gold Flake cigarettes, a tin of golden syrup
and a golden silk handkerchief for neck or
nose. We paid for these with one of the gold
sovereigns which Uncle Godfrey always gave
us when he came to stay.

Our mother's youngest sister, Cicely, sailed
for the Argentine to marry Humphrey
Wykeham Musgrave, who farmed there. We
were so pleased for her and for us: whenever
she came to stay she caused havoc upstairs and
downstairs, in kitchen, pantry, nursery, and
between our mother and father. She was
spiteful, scheming and deceitful. On her last
visit she had explained carefully to me that our
mother and father loved Owen because he
was the only son, and Cynthia because she was

beautiful – but they did not love me at all. 'I am your Godmother – the only one who loves you,' she said. I consulted Nannie Kate about this and she was outraged. 'You are the naughtiest, the most exhausting and the plainest of the family,' she said. But she added generously, 'We all love you and specially because you make us laugh, which is important.' We all felt sorry for Humphrey Wykeham Musgrave. However, she came back like a boomerang! Her husband couldn't cope because she was so difficult. When she came back, she lived for a long time in Cirencester with Grannie and Grandpa. She made a reign of terror for them with her scheming, deceit and disloyalty.

She tried to turn everyone against these nice old people. She would go around the house – where there were a lot of servants in those days, cooks and housemaids, etc. – and she would say to them, 'I don't know why you work here, they are awful to you.' She was a troublemaker, a nasty piece of work.

In March 1921 our father won the Members' Light Weight Race at the Cotswold hunt point-to-point on Wild Monk. We watched from one of the farm wagons which were lined up by the winning post. Owen and I each won a florin.

At last, in May 1921, we moved into Combend. The mile-long lane from the old Roman road had been repaired to make a nice drive; the great barn had become a huge hall with refectory tables and comfortable furniture and an open log fire at one end. Through an archway a wide oak staircase led down to a white panelled drawing room, a dining room, a sitting room and a study, and upstairs to our mother and father's rooms, guest rooms and nurseries. Above the nurseries were two attic rooms for Owen and me. Behind the big hall was a steep, narrow, secret staircase which led

to a tiny sitting room over the high arch of
the barn door: this was to be 'story time room'.

A row of stables – already filled with horses
– and garages lay behind the kitchen area. The
gardens had been laid out and planted, and not
far away – at Sadler's Farm – there were Red
Poll cattle and Berkshire pigs. Chickens, ducks,
turkeys, geese and our bantams lived there
too. We spent all day exploring – thrilled and
happy – while Nannie Kate unpacked. 'No
lodges, no neighbours, no shops . . . we might
be on the moon,' she said.

That evening our great friend and guardian,
Hermes the greyhound, died. Our mother
was desolate and Owen and I cried – we could
not remember life without him. Next morning
we buried him under a holly tree beside the
drive: he still looked beautiful, though he was
all stiff. Owen and I were appalled when our
chauffeur and gardener threw earth over him.
We covered his grave with flowers.

Soon a new governess, Miss Saunders, came to live at Combend. She was tall and pleasant and gave us lessons every morning. We were taught under the Parents National Educational Union scheme and our books and curriculum arrived by post. We enjoyed picture study, history, citizenship and nature study. Already we knew the names of most of the birds, trees and wild flowers from cigarette cards, but we found arithmetic difficult, and so did Miss Saunders.

Once lessons and lunch were over, we were free. Our mother's herd of Welsh mountain ponies, which she had started at Baglan in 1917, was now large – twenty-one ponies in all – and that summer we were each given one foal for our very own. We led them around like dogs, on calves' halters and, when they were strong enough to carry us, we backed them. At first they had to have key bits but later we rode them in snaffles. We groomed and saddled them ourselves but mostly we rode bareback. They were much easier to ride, and faster, than Shetland ponies and we liked to pretend we were Red Indians.

We kept a lot of dogs which had to be exercised. Every day we ran with them across the hills and along the valleys: Hebe and Juno were greyhounds, Dusky, a deer-hound, a collie and a spaniel who belonged to our father; three lurchers belonged to Owen, Cynthia and me; and Deenie, an Aberdeen terrier, was the nursery dog. We also 'walked' four foxhound puppies for Uncle Cecil and two more for the Cotswold hunt. Now and then we took the long dogs out in slips and coursed hares with our mother and father: the chase was thrilling and pretty to watch but we hated the kill. Sometimes we ran all the way to Colesborne post office to buy bull's-eyes – a big paper bag full cost two pence. The postmaster loved our dogs, though they could not all get into his small shop at the same time. He warned us about adders and told us they had a mark like an arrow on their heads and were really dangerous. 'Should any of them dogs be bit, bring them quick to me and I will save them,' he told us. Little Deenie was the first who had to accept this invitation. The postmaster rolled her up in hot leather from head to tail. After two weeks her poor swollen body returned to normal and we were able to fetch her home.

On Sundays we walked across fields with our mother to go to Elkstone Church, which was small and very old. When we got home, there was roast beef for lunch. Once a month our mother took us to see 'the families' – everyone who worked for us. We drove in the pony trap to each cottage with baskets of food, clothes and flowers. We loved these visits and learned a lot about animals, weather, herbs and hardships. She would take things she had knitted, children's clothes and little presents because the working people were very poor. One day we had been around the families delivering food and presents, when suddenly the pony bolted. The cart turned over and we were all thrown out, but we weren't hurt.

The cottagers were very poor. There was no electricity, so each cottage had just a stove and candles with one or two oil lamps. There were awful little upright huts outside each cottage, which were loos and they had to get their water from a well. Mummy and I were always taken into the best parlour rooms when we visited. The cottages always smelt as if the windows hadn't been opened for years. If it was very cold, then a fire was lit for us; it was very formal. The staff called Mummy 'Madam'. They loved her and she was brilliant with them. She looked after everybody within miles

when they were ill and we would go and sit by
the bed of the sick person.

Sometimes, as a treat, we went with Nannie
Kate in the carrier which went once a week
to Cirencester market; it was always crammed
with women and children, pigs, produce,
poultry and fleas.

When we had been at Combend for a few
weeks, Great Uncle Henry arrived one day
on foot with a present under his arm for me:
it was a black lamb from his special flock of
sheep. He had walked four miles from
Colesborne and when he arrived he said to
Mummy, 'I've brought your dear little girl a
present and here it is', and he gave me the
little lamb. Uncle Henry, along with Robin
Hood, was one of Owen's and my heroes.

Visitors came incessantly to stay at
Combend, but story-time remained sacred:
after tea we escaped up the little secret stairway

to spend a whole hour alone with our mother, who read, or told us wonderful stories.

In the branches of the old medlar tree which grew on the lawn at Combend, Owen and I discussed everything and everybody. We knew our cook hated our butler and that Nannie Kate was jealous of Miss Saunders. We talked of the dreadful time when Owen would be sent to prep school; of the baby our mother was expecting; and which cigarette cards we would swap with the stable boys. We collected sets of famous race horses, ships, railway trains and wild flowers. We also talked about the quarrels which occasionally erupted between our father and mother. They seemed to happen because of two things: our father's anxiety to 'toughen up' Owen before he went to boarding school; and extravagance, or *folie de grandeur* as our mother called it.

Our father often challenged Owen to climb to the top of very high trees whose branches

bent even under his small weight, or to walk
through beds of stinging nettles in his shorts,
or ride bareback a pony which had never been
ridden before. Owen was small for his age
because of his illness but he was immensely
brave and never funked these 'dares'. But they
terrified our mother and me and several times
I kicked and bit my father, who smacked me
in return but never relented.

Owen and I only half understood
'extravagance'. We knew our father bought
anything he fancied regardless of cost, that
beautiful cars and presents arrived often,
that the Red Poll bull for which he paid a record
price at Reading Sales had proved to be
impotent, that people gasped when they heard
what he had spent on Combend, but he was
carefree and apparently had no need to worry
about money.

Our mother and father adored each other.
She was always gentle and good natured unless

she was frightened. He was generally immensely kind and generous but he had a terrible temper. Daddy was ambitious for Owen and wanted him to go to Winchester. It shook him to the roots when Owen failed the entrance exam. Daddy was a very kind man but he terribly wanted his only son, who had been reduced to a frail little boy when he should have been playing rugger, to succeed. He had a very loud voice and was terrifying when he was angry. He was proud of Owen and loved him, but he bullied him often. 'Owen must get used to being bullied,' he would say. But none of us understood.

1921

In September 1921 our mother took Owen away to a preparatory boarding school called Summerfields at St Leonards-on-Sea. He wore

(*top*) Godfrey and Dossie Llewellyn on their wedding day, 1920. Dossie wore trousers!

(*left*) Nannie Kate

(*above*) Growing up. Me in 1920

(*opposite top*) Great Uncle Henry Elwes and Great Aunt Margie Elwes on their Golden Wedding Anniversary, 1921

(*opposite bottom*) Owen, Cynthia and me hunting together for the first time with the Cotswold hounds, April 1921

(*above*) Owen, me, Cicely, Cynthia, Kitty and Dorothy at Combend in 1922

(*opposite top*) Combend, 1922

(*opposite bottom*) Daddy and
Owen in the garden,
Cirencester

(*above*) Gran Llewellyn with
her fifteen grandchildren,
Baglan Hall, 1924

(*right*) Gran Llewellyn at
Baglan, 1928

(*opposite*) Mummy, Daphne and Jimmy the monkey, Lausanne, Switzerland, 1930

(*above*) Daddy sailing on Lake Geneva, summer 1931

(*above*) The Garden House, 1929

(*below*) Cynthia and Daphne with Jock and Deanie, 1933

long grey flannel trousers with a matching jacket, a straw boater and a hideous school tie. He had a trunk filled with school uniform, and a tuck box. After the car drove off to take them to the station, Nannie Kate and Cynthia cried and I went and sat for hours in the medlar tree. Our mother returned two days later – she looked tired and sad.

It seemed as if winter came as soon as Owen left. It was bitterly cold at Combend in spite of the central heating. At night the wind howled and moaned over our roof and now I was alone under the rafters. Happy, my lurcher, was no longer allowed to sleep on my bed because he had grown too big. I stole hunks of bread to feed the mice in my bedroom and they grew quite tame.

We went hunting often, either with the Cotswold or Uncle Cecil's hounds. One day I managed to be there for the kill. It was dreadful: everyone whooped and yelled while

the hounds tore the fox to pieces and at the
end the huntsman cut off its head and pads.
Because I was the youngest rider there I was
'blooded' by the Master: he rubbed one of
the fox's bleeding pads on my cheeks and then
gave it to me to put in my pocket. When I
went to bed that night I looked at the little pad
which had run so fast and well, and felt terribly
ashamed. My mother came to kiss me
goodnight and found me crying but I could
not tell her why: she and our father looked so
wonderful when they went out hunting – he
in his top hat and pink coat, and she, tall and
elegant, on her side-saddle. It seemed wrong
that so many people and hounds should chase
one small animal and watch it being torn to
shreds and eaten. The words which inspired
us in story books – chivalry, gallantry and
fair-play – seemed to get forgotten in real
life.

At last, when the Christmas holidays came,

we were able to discover from Owen what
Summerfields was like. In his weekly letter to
our mother he wrote only that he hoped we
were well and happy and that he was well and
happy. Now we learned that he had made a
lot of friends and had settled in well. He taught
me quite a few new words: quis, ego, adsum,
swiz, snubs, sucks and shit.

During those holidays we went to many
children's parties, most of them ten or more
miles away. These were lavish and rather
formal: after we had shaken hands with the
host and hostess we were given small
programmes with tiny pencils attached by
silken cords so that we could write down the
names of our partners for each dance. First
we danced Sir Roger de Coverley and Oranges
and Lemons; after tea we did the waltz and
foxtrot and, finally, the gallop. At one party,
Owen challenged me to see which of us could
eat the most ice-creams. He ate twenty-one

and defeated me. At another, which was fancy dress, I went as a Welsh girl in a top hat, shawl and long wool skirt: it was dreadfully hot and after a while I shed the shawl and skirt. Nannie Kate, sitting with a row of uniformed nannies on gilt and wicker chairs, went scarlet as I waltzed by in my top hat and petticoat. Before we went home, we gathered round a Christmas tree lit by crimson candles and laden with crackers and parcels, and each of us was given a present.

None of the mothers we saw at these parties was as beautiful as ours, nor did any of them seem to possess such magic: she was always surrounded by a throng of laughing children – even tiny ones were never shy of her.

1922

A week before Owen returned to school, our mother had her fourth child – a little girl with blue eyes and brown hair. They dressed her in long, hand-made clothes – all tucks, frills and lace – and named her Daphne.

Because Owen was learning Latin and football at school, I began to try harder at my lessons: I did not want to be left behind. Now Cynthia, three years younger than me and more delicate, was allowed to roam and ride with me and, when the leaves came back on the medlar tree, she joined me in its high branches.

During that spring and summer we took our ponies to gymkhanas and horse shows. The first time out I rode in the Children's Pony Class at the Three Counties Show at

Gloucester on Dynamo, who was two years
old. We won second prize, but Dynamo, a
fast, strong colt, became frightened when
a rosette was fastened to his bridle and people
began to clap; he bolted round the ring and
through the exit into a maze of cattle, shire
horses, produce stalls, farm machinery and the
fun fair and finally came to a halt inside
the gents' lavatory tent, where I hastily
dismounted. Our Welsh mountain ponies won
a lot of prizes and, occasionally, I won the
coveted prize of Best Rider.

In July my mother and father took me to
Summerfields at St Leonards-on-Sea for
Owen's Parents Day. I wore a yellow organdie
dress and won the visitors' race but this
triumph was rather spoilt when I sat down on
a cowpat to watch the boys' obstacle race
which Owen won.

For a fortnight in the long summer holidays,
Owen, Cynthia and I went to stay with Gran

Llewellyn at Baglan. At Port Talbot station crowds of men were standing around singing. 'It's heart-breaking,' said Gran's chauffeur who met us. 'They are still unemployed.' We stopped at the Lower Lodge to hug Old Margaret and then at the Upper Lodge to see Mr and Mrs Poole and Dai. The rooks were cawing and circling on their way to bed. Gran and Lizzie met us at the front door: they looked smaller than we remembered and at night the house seemed dark, with only oil lamps and candles.

Each morning Lizzie drew our curtains, made us wash and dress and be down in time for family prayers. Gran sat at the head of the dining-room table armed with a prayer book and Bible. Then Lizzie led in a procession of maids wearing caps and aprons and carrying two long wooden benches upon which they seated themselves. After Gran had read a text and lesson everyone turned round and knelt while she said prayers. It was difficult not to laugh. Breakfast followed and then we were free to re-explore every room, upstairs and downstairs, the garden, bothy, laundry, stables, the summer house, greenhouses and then race up to the top of the mountain and scramble down the cwm to the marshes and the sea. One day Tom the carpenter and Huw, our policeman, took us on a bus to Port Talbot to see our thief. Another time we visited Aunt Dolly and her goitre, and our handsome boy cousins David and Francis, and their little sister Mary. Their nannie was still wearing her beaded bonnet.

This visit to Baglan was fun but it was also sad. Port Talbot and Briton Ferry had crept closer to Baglan – our wonderful world was shrinking and so were our old friends and Gran. On our way home, at Gloucester station, we searched for the Airedale dog who begged for charity, but the station master told us he was dead. Back in the medlar tree we agreed that when Gran died, Baglan would end and even the rooks would leave.

1923

When autumn came, Cynthia and I went cubbing with Hicks, our gloomy groom, who never looked at anything except his horse's ears. He missed seeing hedgehogs, foxes, squirrels, weasels, rabbits, hares and, sometimes, badgers. The country looked wonderful as the sun came up and lit cobwebs in the grass and undergrowth. Every bird seemed to be singing and some called a warning when they heard our ponies' hooves thudding along. We arrived home in time for breakfast, which we ate slowly so as to be late for lessons.

It was never dull at Combend and we had many excitements: one day our father caused a sensation out hunting because, when the hounds 'found', he jumped the tall, double level-crossing gates to get over the main railway line; his horse, Disguise, never refused anything. On another, when all our dogs were chasing a cat, our collie, Don, collided with our mother in the stable yard and bit a huge chunk out of her leg and ate it. We went to the Cirencester 'Mop', a fair in the market place, where we played hoop-la for goldfish and won coconuts shooting in a rifle range; we went to a cinema for the first time – to see *Felix the Cat*. It was an awful little building. We thought it was too wonderful for words. We couldn't believe it. We got in for about sixpence. It was very simple inside but we didn't mind. There were benches and chairs to sit on and somebody played the harmonium during the interval.

Often we picnicked at Lyde, a lake above Colesborne, where Mr and Mrs Belcher lived in a thatched cottage – he wore a beard and a top hat and told us how he went out by moonlight to collect herbs to make into medicines. Geoffrey Bruce, who had recently climbed up Mount Everest, came to stay; it was exciting sitting by the fire in the big hall listening to his icy stories. Catherine Mayer, the artist, returned – this time to paint a portrait of Cynthia. A new popular song delighted Nannie Kate and she sang it every morning as she curled Daphne's hair into long ringlets with damp rags:

Ka-Ka-Katie – beautiful Katie.
   You're the only girl who I adore.
When the mo-mo-moon shines
   Over the co-co-cow sheds
I'll be waiting at the ki-ki-kitchen door.

Now we could jump quite high stone walls on our ponies and our saddle room was festooned with rosettes. Our father was kept

busy with the farm and he and our mother
went out often to hunt, shoot, course, fish,
race and go to balls – yet they spent a great
deal of time with us. Life was carefree and
happy – and as each season came we loved it
better than the last: spring with its small
flowers, birds' nests, buds and blossoms;
summer, when a sea of roses came out in the
garden and our ponies' coats shone brighter
than our furniture, and mown lawns smelt
good. Autumn brought us fruit and berries
and stubble fields where we could gallop fast
and jump bales of straw or ride on the farm
wagons and watch the trees turning from green
to gold; yet still we loved winter – the snow
and ice, the gales and downpours, and evenings
beside blazing log fires.

Christmas 1923 seemed extra special;
Grannie, Grandpa, Gran and all our uncles
and aunts came to stay. Our ages ranged from
one year old to eighty. The Christmas tree

looked taller and more splendid than ever and our presents were wonderful. One night our mother and father gave a party for everyone who worked for us – in the house and on the land – and the next night they gave a ball for friends and neighbours. We were allowed to stay up late on both evenings. We did not learn that these were farewell parties until all our visitors had departed.

Our mother told us. We'd raced up the secret stairs to the story-time room and found her looking so pretty in a tea-gown, with a leather-bound copy of *Huckleberry Finn* on her lap. She began to read but suddenly tears streamed down her cheeks and then, with difficulty, she said: 'Combend has been sold – our house and land. The cattle, sheep, pigs, nearly all the horses, ponies and dogs must be given away or sold . . . even the poultry must go. Soon we must say goodbye to nearly everyone who works for us . . .' 'Why, why,

why?' we asked, but she wept so much she could not answer. Nor did she ever answer that question — to any of us.

Combend was sold because my father had spent too much money and had no idea at all of the value of anything. He wanted to have a big estate, a superb herd of cattle and hunters, and steeplechase horses. He never asked the price of anything, he just plunged himself into debt.

As we were going to bed that night, Cynthia, who was seven, announced that no one could sell her pony, her dog or Nannie Kate and, wherever we might go, we must take the medlar tree with us. When I was alone in my bedroom with the mice, I cried myself to sleep.

1924

In the New Year we looked at everything with
anxious eyes: the days of reckoning had begun.
What should be sold, given away or kept?
Owen, Cynthia and I trailed around behind
our parents listening to the verdicts on
everything and, as these decisions were
implemented, day after day there were terrible
departures. Our mother never grumbled or
blamed and our father kept up his attractive
laughing bravado but all of us felt miserable,
except for Nannie Kate, who could not conceal
her joy that we might move to 'somewhere
more civilized'. On our own territory – in the
nursery and schoolroom – we had blazing
rows with her as she tried faithfully to reduce
our toys and clutter and pack 'real necessities'
into trunks. 'Your conkers must be thrown

out; you can collect some more next year. You have thousands of cigarette cards; give them to the stable boys. You are too old to keep a rocking horse; he must be given away.' The battle for Dapple, our rocking horse, lasted for days and only when we all refused to eat did the grown-ups surrender. Whenever Nannie Kate went into the night nursery to put Daphne to bed, we rushed to the day nursery to bury our treasures deep in the trunks she had been packing.

It was decided that our mother's greyhound, Cynthia's lurcher and little Deenie be kept, and our mother's beautiful chestnut hunter, Tirpanda, and three ponies – all the rest would be sold or given away. And so, one dreadful afternoon, Mr Newey, a race-horse trainer from Cleeve Hill, arrived and drove off with Happy, my beloved dog. I minded so much that I could not look at anybody, talk of it, or

even cry. Day after day our happiness seemed
to disintegrate.

On 17 March, when all was settled, we
drove slowly, like a funeral cortège, along our
drive, past Hermes' grave, to the Roman road,
where we turned left for Cirencester. No one
spoke. I felt sick and sad and also
uncomfortable: I had hidden two of my mice
and four Roman snails in small cardboard boxes
in my knickers; for once it helped that I was
rather plump.

1924–7

We disliked Dollar Street House, Cirencester,
before we got out of the car. It was a 'pavement
house', three storeys high. It had a small walled
garden at the back and adjoining it was a yard
with a garage, two loose boxes and a

greenhouse. Inside the house, a staircase led from the front hall to the third-floor nurseries, where a high wire cage surrounded the stairwell so that we could not lean over the banisters. The rooms were high and square with big sash windows. Some people might have thought it a nice house but we did not. At the end of Dollar Street was the beautiful Cirencester church but its bells pealed loud and often and always depressed us.

For weeks after we left Combend, I had nightmares: I dreamed that I was being sold along with the pigs and sheep. Perhaps it was lucky Owen and I no longer slept under the rafters – when I screamed or shouted in the night, Nannie Kate heard and came to comfort me. She was amazed to find mice in my bedroom and told Cook that Gloucestershire was unusually bad for vermin.

A new governess came to give me lessons – a hideous woman with bad breath, but she made my lessons fascinating, so I liked her and learned well. We rode regularly in Cirencester Park – it was boring just going up and down its long and beautiful rides with nothing to jump. Sometimes we went hunting with Lord Bathurst's hounds but this too was tame compared with the Cotswold hunt.

Nannie Kate took us for ghastly pavement walks – she seemed to know the owner of every corner shop in town and stopped to gossip. One night Owen had a row with her in the nursery: 'We've lost our freedom. Who cares about luxury and comfort? At Baglan and Combend we were free, but here you tell us that we cannot run or ride alone because we do not know the neighbours; you implore us to stay on the pavements lest we be run over; and when we go into this or that field you say we are trespassing.' There was a pause and then Owen shouted, 'You do not understand freedom. It is something no one can live without or buy but everyone needs. It is as precious as life itself – lots of people die for it.' For once Nannie Kate did not answer but her hair fell down and, from habit and affection, we all stooped to pick up her hairpins. Owen's face was pink with rage when suddenly our mother came in and asked what was going on. 'We were talking about the Kingdom of Heaven,' Owen said defiantly. Our mother looked at each of us in turn – level and stern. 'The Kingdom of Heaven is wherever you may be if you make it so. Whether you live in a tent, an igloo, a castle, in town or country – it can be heaven, but it is up to you. Never forget that, and please never ever shout again at Nannie Kate, or anyone else.' When she had gone, we looked up 'igloo' in our dictionary. It said, 'dome-shaped hut, especially one built of snow.' 'No need for hairpins in an igloo,' Owen told Nannie Kate. 'In that sort of home your hair would be frozen stiff and stay up.' He kissed her gently and told her he would explain freedom to her another time. When we went to bed that night, Nannie Kate was especially nice to us. 'The only thing that matters is that we all stay together. If we ever get separated it will be ghastly,' she said.

Except for Nannie Kate, none of us enjoyed living in Cirencester: we felt restless and were no longer carefree. Our father worked hard in our small garden and seemed to get pleasure from throwing slugs and snails over the wall into our neighbour's garden. The rest of the time he drove our mother around in his Rolls. He gave up riding. The fashion changed and now our mother wore short dresses with skirts above her knees, often with a fringe along the hem. Her waist moved south and seemed to encircle her bottom. We missed her long, swishing, graceful skirts. She hunted on Tirpanda with Lord Bathurst's hounds. In his holidays Owen was bored until he acquired a bicycle, on which he pedalled far and wide and caused anxiety by returning late night after night.

After reading *The Scarlet Pimpernel*, *Beau Geste* and *Bulldog Drummond*, Cynthia and I decided to create our own secret society. Carefully we wrote down its rules:

1. No grown-up may know of it – or belong to it.
2. Its aims: To fight cruelty to animals and birds.
   To rebel against governesses and milk puddings.
   To be nicer to ugly people.
   To read more and ride better.

We had discovered a trap door in the ceiling of the housemaids' cupboard which let us on to the roof. Once we'd hoisted each other up, we found we could walk along Dollar Street three floors above the pavement, within a small ledge. We made our office there and equipped it with necessities: candles, matches, pens, paper, a few books and biscuits. It was our triumph that now we could vanish, escape grown-ups and be private.

For many months we enjoyed this freedom until some boring woman spotted us on the roof and told our parents. Then the trap door to the roof was nailed up. We created other hide-outs – in the hay loft, in the cellar, and under the main staircase, but sooner or later they were all discovered and invaded by grown-ups who removed our candles, matches and maps. Considering our efforts to be polite to so many of their boring guests at our house, this behaviour seemed to us unfair and rude.

Our mother sometimes gave us special treats. One of the best was to go and see the rodeo when it came to London. It was wonderful. There were so many people at Wembley that we could hardly get in. I didn't learn for years that string was tied around the loins of the horses so the poor devils kicked and kicked and kicked – they couldn't do anything else. We thought they were wild horses.

Our days were seldom boring: so often things happened to surprise or amuse us all. One day, our fat cook advanced on our mother, looking grim. We thought she was about to give notice. But she explained she had sat on a darning needle which was now emerging from her groin. She said she would be obliged if our mother would pull it out, whereupon she lifted up her clothes and exposed her dreadful underneath. Our mother, undaunted, pulled out a bodkin. It was thick and sharp and must have been painful. Our cook was jubilant to have it removed and kept it as a souvenir in a small velvet frame beside our cooker.

After a while I was sent to a day school in the town, where I learned very little but soon noticed that if I was nice to the headmistress's revoltingly fat and smelly dog, I got high marks for my work. This resulted in people thinking I was clever and I was put down to take the Junior Oxford Exam at Oxford. Petrified by being dispatched to stay with strangers in Oxford and sit in a university hall, I hardly put pen to paper and failed in all subjects.

I was given one day away from school to have lunch with Mummy at Grannie and Grandpa's, when suddenly Mummy was very nasty to me for no reason. I couldn't understand why she turned on me; I was stunned and I put my head on the table and started to cry and I couldn't stop. I was still crying that evening; I was having hysterics. I have a feeling that Granny and Grandpa realized then that my mother was not all right.

1928

Quite suddenly, in 1928, our father bought a
pretty Queen Anne house in Berkshire. It was
called the Garden House and was on the edge
of a village called Stanford Dingley.

It had a nice garden bordering a mill stream.
Immediately he began building on a wing. Our
mother, who worried about money and was
trying to economize, was upset by this
extravagance, and once again quarrels began.

My mother adored Daddy but I think she
was frightened about the amount of money
he was spending and she hated it when he
showed off with money. I often thought
secretly that it was all too much for her and
that it sent her out of her mind. She became
frightened. 'Perhaps both of them are having
the "change of life",' said Nannie Kate. Now

she was our only help: she cooked, cleaned and grumbled in her good-natured way.

Suddenly Mummy had become different – she kept going to stay with people we had never heard of who she had known before she was married – it was almost invisible to start with and then it grew more blatant. I think my mother became difficult – Daddy had spoiled her over a long period. She had always been so lovely and soft and sweet, and when she attacked me at that lunch on my one day off from school, I was stunned: she changed and suddenly became tougher.

The first time we children noticed that something was really wrong in our family was when we were told we would not be together for Christmas: Cynthia and Daphne would go with our mother to Grannie Elwes in Gloucestershire and Owen and I would go with our father to stay with Grannie Llewellyn in Wales. Owen said to me, 'That arrangement is the end of a happy Christmas.'

Before we left for Wales, we went Christmas shopping with our mother. She said, 'I must buy something small for dear Griff', and she bought him a book called *Goodbye to All That*, by Robert Graves. In Wales we went Christmas shopping with our father. He said, 'I must buy something small for dear Con', and bought her a book called *A Farewell to Arms*, by Ernest Hemingway. Owen and I tried hard to understand this behaviour but never thought, for one moment, that we were watching the end of a happy family.

My great friend, Grannie Elwes, who may have noted that things were going wrong in our family, insisted on providing money for me to be sent to a better school and I was despatched to Southover Manor School in Lewes, Sussex.

Winifred Ponsonby had started up Southover School. She was a very clever woman who decided that it would be a good idea for families not to have a governess for their children but to have several governesses in one place where all the children could go. This became a school. It was in a rather nasty house, between a main road and a railway, with two playing fields, but it made an excellent school.

Perhaps because I'd sat for the Junior Oxford Exam I was put in a class of girls older than me. Though my uniform and pocket money, much to my embarrassment, were inadequate, I was lucky to be the fastest runner in the school and so was placed in the hockey, lacrosse and tennis teams. For away matches, with much laughter, my friends kitted me out in the hideous correct uniform: brown knickers, tunic and blazer.

It was a nice school with charming teachers and I learnt a lot. Every Sunday I went to lunch with my Ponsonby cousins who lived nearby. They were all very good-looking and fun too.

Miss Roberts, the headmistress of Southover, was known as Roary because, whatever happened, she always burst into tears: if you were had up for misbehaviour she'd say, 'Oh, my child, how could you be so stupid? How dreadful. I'll have to punish you, which I've no wish to do.' And then she'd burst into tears. If you'd done something good, she'd demand to see you: 'Oh, my child, two goals and good marks in geography. How wonderful you are', and tears ran down her cheeks. If you were lucky, she'd say, 'I'm having crumpets for tea and would be proud if you'd join me.' Sadly this nice fat woman retired and was succeeded by a very good-looking young South African woman who flayed us with a vicious tongue and hated some of the girls, of whom I was one.

There was a girl at Southover called Mary

whom we couldn't help loving. She would
start to laugh and the whole school laughed.
She was as mad as a hatter. One day we were
all sitting in a French lesson, when she suddenly
rose out of her chair and picked up our tiny
bow-legged French mistress, flung her over her
shoulder and walked out of the classroom.
Eventually she came back without
Mademoiselle. Days passed and nobody could
find Mademoiselle. We were all worried
because we wondered if Mary had killed her!
There was a huge recreation room where we
had roll call every morning – the elder girls
sat at the back and the little ones were at the
front. Some of the older girls thought they
could hear a strange tapping at the back of this
room where there was a lavatory and they
insisted on going and seeing what this noise
was. It was Mademoiselle – she had been there
for several days. Mary said, 'She was all right.
There was plenty of water in the loo and she

could eat the loo paper, which is really made from vegetables.' She was eventually expelled.

As well as our French mistress and Roary the headmistress, we had Bunny, who was our matron. She was simply marvellous. I was surviving quite well at school, when all letters from home stopped. As the weeks passed, I grew frightened. I told no one and bottled up increasing fear that something appalling had happened. Perhaps my anxious mind poisoned my body: huge carbuncles appeared on my thighs and before long I could not walk or run normally. When one burst, it was so enormous and frightful that it hit the ceiling. It was full of the most dreadful poison and it hurt like mad. At last I pulled myself together and went to Bunny and asked her to have a look at my legs. She was appalled. I was removed to the sanatorium in great pain. Bunny insisted I tell her what I was thinking about. She said one's mind can affect one's body. Eventually I told her. She telephoned my grandparents. They said that my mother and father had separated; our house was closed; my mother was seriously ill in a hospital in Bristol; my little sisters, with Kate, were with an uncle in Wales; no one knew where my father was; Owen was still at school. When the holidays began I must go straight to my grandparents. Devastated, I waited for my legs to heal.

When I arrived from school to stay with Grannie Elwes in Cirencester, I was told Aunt Cicely would drive me in the morning to see my mother at the hospital in Bristol. It was a long drive to Bristol and Aunt Cicely exuded poisonous remarks about my grandparents until I pretended to go to sleep. We arrived at a large and rather grim building and were taken through endless locked doors until we reached my mother's room. I was appalled to find her looking ill, frightened and unkempt. I tried to find out who had taken her there and

by whose authority but she was too frail
and confused to tell me. Leaving her was
ghastly. Hardly had I got back into my Aunt's
car when she said, 'I hope you realize that was
a lunatic asylum.'

Back in Grannie's house I tried to be cheerful
because the two old people were piteously
awaiting good news but as soon as I could
escape I went to bed, locked my door and,
after releasing my enormous grief, began to
think and plot. It seemed that after my mother
and father parted, she became desperately
depressed and doctors came and took her away
to Bristol. But by whose authority and how?
Before I fell asleep, I determined to go to a
call-box in the morning and contact my father
at Baglan.

My father acted like lightning. He opened
up the Garden House and re-installed Nannie
Kate with my little sisters and fetched our
mother from Bristol. He filled the house with

food and flowers and collected Owen and me.
Our father was sure he could rescue and mend
our mother by sheer love. We took great care
of her when she was depressed and sad, and
when she became angry and eccentric we did
not recognize that this was illness but just
thought that she was over-tired and irritable.
For a long time none of us realized that she
was very ill, the victim of a dreadful disease
(doctors later described her as a manic
depressive). Perhaps our father recognized this
after a while, but we children did not
understand that our mother's ups and downs
were not normal.

She would meet strangers and send them to
stay with us and she would get so depressed
that she wouldn't get out of bed in the morning
or dress herself. We used to try to get her
dressed and would say, 'Mummy here are your
knickers.' 'Oh.' 'Well, darling Mummy could
you try and put them on?' 'No.' 'Well,

Mummy, let me put them on for you.' And it would go on like that. It was too awful for words. Then she'd become more normal, would put on hat and coat and go off to London to visit the Ritz and buy extravagant things. But nothing ever stopped all of us from adoring her.

During those long summer holidays my mother steadily recovered. Our father was wonderful to her and we were all thankful and happy to be together again. Our garden seemed to rejoice too: myriads of flowers bloomed and we decked the house with them. Suddenly it seemed we were once again a happy family.

1929, 1930

On returning home from school for the Christmas holidays in 1928, when I was fifteen,

I found, to my horror, that everything had changed. Physically my mother was fit and well but she was unhappy and constantly furious with one or other of us. My father and Nannie Kate were exhausted and anxious and my little sisters confused and tearful. Before I'd unpacked, my father told me to be ready to leave early next morning for Switzerland. 'That's where the best doctors are,' he said. 'We must go and live there until your mother is cured. You must come and help me buy a villa and consult specialists.'

The train journey to Lausanne was ghastly. My father had not slept well for weeks and seemed to me to be on the edge of a nervous breakdown. Either he sat silently with tears sliding down his cheeks or talked in a torrent about the difficult situation he'd lived through over the past months. He and I always got on very well, so I was happy to keep him company on the trip. While we were in Switzerland, we stood on a bridge over a crevasse in Lausanne and he said, 'I'll make myself throw myself over here.' I was terrified.

High above Lausanne, on the edge of a forest, was a suburb called Vennes. I don't know how he did it, but Daddy bought a large and beautiful new villa there with a superb view over Lake Geneva to the French side. He bought it to please Mummy. It was a nice place for her to recuperate whilst seeing the best doctors. We visited several eminent and charming doctors and then returned to England, where he arranged for some of our mother's favourite furniture to be shipped to Lausanne. Then he closed down the Garden House, gave our ponies and dogs away, telephoned a few of our family to say *au revoir* and away we went.

Our departure was not easy: favourite toys had to be left behind, and we were all upset over parting with our dogs and ponies. Nannie Kate was in a dither because she knew no

French and anyway thought of 'abroad' as dangerous enemy territory. Our mother seemed pleased to go but she criticized all our father's arrangements. Remembering his recent catastrophic extravagance, I wondered how he could afford this new venture but dared not inquire. Somehow we made the long train journey and reached our new home.

At first our new surroundings seemed to calm and please all the family, and for a little while we were happy. But Mummy became peculiar and wasn't very nice to my father – he became shattered by this. All he wanted was for the best doctors to cure her.

Soon after we arrived, our mother discovered a pet shop in Lausanne and returned home one day with a monkey called Jimmy. He was nearly as tall as Daphne. He adored our mother, was civil to us children, but he hated our father and Kate. For a start he bespattered our mother's bedroom with her red nail polish and toothpaste. Then his feud with our father and Nannie Kate spiralled and he hurled food, books and ornaments at them along with a furious chatter of incomprehensible abuse. If anyone scolded him he growled, sat down, took aim, and peed on them. He seemed never to be tired and, by day and night, pounced from behind furniture and doors on all of us and ricocheted between fury and affection. He stole our clothes and wore them; he stole our food and ate it; and he moved furniture around, upstairs and down. Soon our father insisted he be returned to the shop he came from but our mother opposed this and, once again, quarrels began.

After Christmas our mother became more seriously ill and our nights became terrible. When it grew dark she had hallucinations and thought dreadful creatures were crawling across the walls and ceiling of her bedroom.

She dared not go to sleep lest they harm her. Sometimes her fears were so vivid that I too felt afraid. My father and I took turns to sit up all night in her bedroom to try and comfort and reassure her, but gradually we both grew exhausted from lack of sleep and our great concern for her. Eventually our kind and clever Swiss doctor persuaded our father and mother that she should move to a nursing home at Nyon on Lake Geneva.

My father's grief was terrible to see. Nothing could console him. Nannie Kate continued to clean and cook as if her life depended on it. A great pall of sadness descended upon us. Owen had to return to Bradfield College. My two little sisters, who did not understand the situation at all and missed our mother dreadfully, turned to me to help them. If it rained, we played Happy Families, Snap, Beggar My Neighbour, and Hunt the Thimble. If it was fine weather, I took them for long walks in the wonderful forests above Vennes and then they insisted I tell them stories all the way. I started to become a mother figure to Cynthia and Daphne. They both hero-worshipped me. We would all get in a train on the edge of Lake Geneva and go to Nyon to see Mummy. It was lovely until we had to go home and leave her there. We would cry when we left her.

After a while, our mother's eldest sister, the forever kind and amusing Aunt Mary, came from England to see her and cheer us up. She introduced us to a charming American family called Anderson who were in Switzerland to try to cure Mr Anderson of a serious drink problem. All of his family were exceptionally good-looking, and Mr Anderson, who came often to our house, was disarmingly funny. He'd arrive and say, 'Sorry to bother you, but I think I hid a bottle in your sitting room and I've come to collect it.' Then he'd lift every cushion and seat to no avail and retreat to search elsewhere.

Mrs Anderson and Aunt Mary worried about me because I was nearly grown up and never had any fun, so one evening they arranged that their governess and two young Englishmen who were staying with them should take me out to dine and dance in Montreux. The young men were very amusing and we all ate a good dinner before they whisked us round the dance floor of a chic nightclub. It was fun until, quite suddenly, they began hurling china and chairs through the plate-glass window of the nightclub. Glass and bits of furniture flew in every direction, other customers panicked and fled, waiters disappeared and soon the pretty little premises were a shambles. Police arrived, picked the glass out of my hair and escorted us home. There followed a dreadful rumpus: the governess was sacked; the two young men were sent home to England in disgrace; and, having been only a terrified spectator, I was sent to bed.

It was dreadful when the day came for Aunt Mary to go home. She got herself packed and dressed. She had her hat and everything on, when suddenly she decided she wanted a bath. She immediately took everything off except her hat and had a bath. She looked very funny.

Soon after Aunt Mary went home, my father received a letter from Aunt Muriel Elwes at Colesborne in Gloucestershire, inviting me to stay for three months: 'Hermione must now be nearly grown up and it might help her and you if she came and stayed here with Gerda and Bou, who are only slightly older. She would meet a lot of people, go to dances, and hunt.' This letter petrified me. How could I leave my mother and father in their distress? What would become of Cynthia and Daphne – their walks, stories and games? I had no tidy clothes, and anyhow did not want to be a Cinderella in anybody's house. But my father was adamant and insisted I go.

Nannie Kate made me put my hair up in a bun, 'so as to look older', but it fell down if I moved an inch. I packed a little suitcase, was put on a train along with my terror and arrived back in the world we'd left behind.

I'd forgotten much of how we used to live: chauffeurs, butlers, grooms, changing for dinner, five-course meals, four-poster beds, hats and gloves, and pretty dresses. Aunt Muriel riffled through my little suitcase and whisked me off to London, where she bought me suits, dresses, sweaters, shoes, evening clothes, riding clothes and even a fur jacket. Her generosity was overwhelming and I found it impossible to thank her adequately. Her family and indoor and outdoor staff were divine to me; no one allowed me to feel, for a moment, that I was a Cinderella. Soon I was caught up in their busy social life with little time to mope, but however late we went to bed each night I wrote a letter to my family in Switzerland.

One day we were taken to London to see a play called *Journey's End*. It was about the war. I'd never really thought about the war or imagined what it must have been like, so this play gave me a great shock. Everyone in the audience cried – even grown-ups – and on the long drive home no one spoke. When I went to bed that night I cried some more and knew I'd remember the play as long as I lived.

My cousins, Gerda and Bou, and their elder sister, Cecilia, were great fun and very kind to me, and eccentric Uncle Cecil was endlessly surprising and amusing. I loved them all but Aunt Muriel was my favourite: in her quiet way she took care of everything and everybody. She walked over the hills regularly to visit her old mother-in-law, who was frail and lonely. I thought that, if I ever grew old, I'd try to be like her.

After many months of this luxurious life a crisis arose: the exchange rate of the Swiss franc altered and my father had to sell the Swiss villa and valuable furniture and return to England, so I left my cousins to help him open up the Garden House and install the family there. It was heart-rending to leave our mother in the nursing home in Switzerland.

Back at Stanford Dingley we were short of everything – particularly money and furniture. As our dogs and ponies had been given away before we went abroad, life seemed dull. There was no one to give lessons to Cynthia and Daphne, so I tried to cope with this. Nannie Kate, valiantly, remained to cook and clean the house but Owen had to leave his school from lack of funds. Our father, overwhelmed with grief, regret and remorse, became irritable and fierce but occasionally he emerged to drive around in his Rolls-Royce as if to show the world a brave face. Somehow I kept my two little sisters happy by collecting wild flowers, reading stories and playing games but, at bedtime, they always asked for our mother and sobbed when I explained she could not come. This was a very sad time.

One sunny morning when Cynthia, Daphne and I were lying on our bank of the mill stream watching minnows and trout, we heard laughter outside the mill and saw two young men watching the mill rush. We crawled along our narrow bank of the river and, coated with mud, introduced ourselves: 'I'm Hermione, aged sixteen, this is Cynthia, aged thirteen, and this is Daphne, aged eight.' They were charming to us, showed us their mill and took us beyond it, upstream, to see their pretty river-side garden and house, which was filled with lovely books, modern paintings, a printing press, good furniture and music. A Chow dog and a friendly old cook also welcomed us. At lunch time we raced for home but before we left, being entranced by these new friends, we asked if we might sometimes visit them again. We forgot to ask their names.

Before long, a fat, bossy female neighbour arrived to see our father and warn him we'd been seen with two 'queers' in the village and were in deadly danger. Our father did not like the fat lady and immediately invited our new friends to dinner. He liked them. They were called Bob Gathorne-Hardy and Kyrle Leng, and from then on they changed our lives. They introduced us to Virginia Woolf's and Lytton Strachey's books; Augustus John's and Henry Lamb's paintings; classical and jazz music; and they taught us how to take good photographs. They showed us how to use their printing press and allowed us to row their boat. Sometimes they took us to the cinema in Newbury to see the Marx Brothers, or for a picnic on the

Thames. Miraculously they lifted our gloom and helped us to enjoy life again and laugh.

Bob and Kyrle were fascinating. I think Kyrle was the best-looking man I ever saw in my life. He was an Adonis and we all fell in love with him, but Bob and Kyrle were in love with each other. Village life was seldom dull. Even the parson contributed to our amusement. A known drunkard, one Sunday, in the middle of his sermon, there was a loud pop, and froth spurted out of his breast pocket and cascaded over the pulpit on to the aisle. He fled back to his rectory, clutching a burst beer bottle, to the applause and laughter of the congregation.

Soon Owen and I became increasingly worried about our poverty, so we decided to try to earn money. He joined the Empire Air Force and I went to London to find work. I think Owen went into the air force because it was the new thing, the third force, and he did so love flying. He used to fly over our house nearly removing the chimney pots. As he had always been challenged by my father, he became a daredevil.

On my first day in London I walked up and down Bond Street and asked at every shop for a job. Under a barrage of slammed doors and ruderies I retreated. At a dinner party that evening I explained what had happened and someone said, 'Why don't you try the Gas, Light and Coke Company?' – which I'd never heard of. Next morning I set out for this mysterious firm in Horseferry Road near the Thames Embankment. A kind and charming Director of Personnel offered me a job selling gas appliances in their basement at 30 shillings a week. I grabbed this, donned one of their hideous staff dresses and went underground to say to all comers, 'Yes, Madam, may I help you?' I hadn't a clue about the job because I hadn't cooked before – I had hardly been in our kitchen at home. We had always had staff and so I had never learnt to cook and suddenly I found myself selling gas cookers and gas fires. I couldn't say 'Of course it does this, that and the other', so I was soon telling customers, 'If you want to commit suicide comfortably get a big oven so you can do it in comfort or you can roast your mother-in-law!' Amazingly I sold many cookers and fires, to the mirth and astonishment of the other staff and myself.

The basement staff were charming and kind to me. They were amused that I had never been on the underground or on top of a London bus and they giggled over my reluctance to light gas fires and cookers. One of them seemed to be in the same predicament as me because her family had fallen on hard times. She was Blanche Arundell, small, blonde and determined. She invited me for a weekend at her home in the country and we squeezed into her brother's small sports car. On arrival at Wardour Castle we found their parents huddled beside the kitchen stove trying to keep warm. The ruins of the old castle were in the grounds but this large and later building, which was well furnished, was hardly used. Lord and Lady Arundell had no staff as far as I could see. I slept in a huge four-poster bed along with Blanche. As meals were sparse I went in the morning to the nearest village shop and bought a large bag of doughnuts to stop our tummies rumbling. It was an interesting but sad weekend because the situation seemed so hopeless: such a wealth of property and land but lack of funds to care for them, and no one was happy, optimistic or really working. This proud Arundell family were hanging on to the past with little hope for the future. I returned to London feeling sad.

I lived at 9 Paultons Square, Chelsea, in a bedsit when I got my first job. There was a dull woman called Cooie Lane who owned the house and let me a horrible bedroom with breakfast. It was not a dull world: high spirits and laughter cropped up everywhere. Fashions came and went, gossip ran riot, but generally it was amiable and kind. It was an optimistic and happy time. Most of us went to church on Sundays, returned home for Christmas and Easter and followed all kinds of sport on radio or – if we could get there – on the course. The kindness of all age groups was remarkable. England was at peace and each season looked more beautiful than the last. I was no longer 'that girl is quite nice, but she works', as now nearly everyone worked.

Sadly there remained dreadfully poor people, most of whom had large families, and unemployment added to their misery. Their homes were piteous but their courage amazing. Many of the things we now take for granted existed then only for the well-off. Earthen closets, candle light, washing clothes in rivers, walking miles to school and back, inadequate food, clothing, heating and transport were the lot of the less lucky. Decent rich tried hard to help their poorer neighbours, which caused goodwill – especially on large estates – but it was a drop in the ocean compared to the need.

Today, when the availability of public transport, plumbing, heating, schooling, medical help, refrigeration and entertainment have improved for nearly everyone, few can remember what poverty used to mean. It was appalling and is best forgotten, though no one should ever forget the brave and silent struggle of those who suffered it and somehow survived.

This was an era of non-stop change. Skirts moved up and down; a new word became current: divorce. More and more cars appeared on our roads and horse-drawn vehicles began to vanish along with candles and oil-lamps.

People began to travel in aeroplanes. Homes became warmer because of central heating and were no longer just cottages, houses and castles, but now there were also flats, bedsits, bungalows and caravans. Buttons and hooks were eclipsed by zip fasteners; calling cards vanished, along with veils, bowler hats and servants' halls. Woolworths arrived and, soon after, supermarkets. Many wealthy people now worked long hours and some handed over their beautiful homes to the National Trust. The poor became safer, bolstered by government money, especially if unemployed. Sport remained our nation's greatest interest and pleasure.

Our famous little country had won the world war against tremendous odds, backed by Canada, Australia and New Zealand. Our language and democracy had spread around the world and our Commonwealth grew. We were admired, envied and often hated. Our

public still paid more attention to the Derby,
the Grand National and, of course, football,
than to anything else. Our cars, bloodstock,
literature, men's suits, furniture, gardens and
many other things were still the best in the
world, and against a background of an
incredibly beautiful land, we seemed to saunter
along with only a few strikes, epidemics and
snobberies to deter us. Britain was not called
'Great' for nothing.

One Saturday afternoon, when I got home
from London by bus, train and walking, I
found a little letter addressed to me on the hall
table. It was from my father. It came from the
Savoy Hotel, Funchal, Madeira. He wrote that
he had eloped with Betty Karslake, the
daughter of an old widow who lived in Stanford
Dingley within a few hundred yards of us.
Betty's brother, who was divorced, also lived
there. He took a terrific shine to me and
behaved very badly, as I was very young for

him to be going round with. He had a nice
Wolseley Hornet car and he used to say,
'Where I shall drive you today?' I thought it
was marvellous. Daddy used to go and see the
Karslakes as good neighbours quite often. But
we had no idea that he was going to do a bunk
with Betty.

He wrote that after living alone for nearly
seven years – because of our mother's illness
– he could not bear it any more. Doctors had
warned him that it was unlikely our mother
would ever fully recover. Meanwhile he had
fallen in love with Betty Karslake. He hoped
my sisters and I would try to understand.
It was a sensitive and rather tragic letter
which ended up: 'Of course I can never
love anyone so much as I loved your
mother.'

I was stunned but after a while I began to
laugh. Then I began to cry and wept as never
before. I sent him a telegram to Madeira: 'Can

just understand stop Maybe Mummy will too
stop What will become of your children
stop Love Hermione.' Then I sat down to
try and think what could or should happen
next.

1933–6

Though we were the children of lucky and
privileged parents and knew a lot about nature
– wild birds and animals, trees, flowers, crops
and insects – our education by charming but
ignorant nannies and governesses left us ill-
prepared for life beyond the boundaries of a
country estate. When our father squandered
his fortune and one by one we set off for
London to earn our living, we were poorly
equipped to fend for ourselves: we had only
good English and good manners to recommend
us. Laughter saved us. Cynthia, three years

younger than me, beautiful, frail and marvellously absent-minded, was loved and helped by everyone. She had the art of crying instantly if anything was difficult or boring: she'd just sit down and sob, whereupon everyone would leap to help her – do her job or pay her share of whatever. Not so attractive, I depended upon extra energy and no regard for hours of work.

At first the noise of London appalled me and so did the underground and the rush hour. Soon I got blisters from walking on pavements. I was embarrassed because I owned no clothes suitable for city life – neither at work nor socially. I was frequently hungry because I was apt to spend my small wages on going to a cinema, a play or a museum rather than buy food. I went out for dinner with people I didn't particularly like in order to get a meal. My rented bedsit was hideous and not comfortable. Yet I was happy and people of all ranks were kind to me. Gradually I explored London and occasionally moved to jobs for more money, shorter hours and greater interest.

After a while I was offered a slightly better paid job on the *Spectator*, provided I could learn shorthand and typing in three months. I achieved this with difficulty and became secretary to Sir Evelyn Wrench, but the hours were exhausting and so was he, and, after learning that government offices only worked from 10 a.m. to 4 p.m., I moved to the War Office where, in a vast room, under the strict surveillance of a severe lady called Miss Roads, I typed dispatches along with a lot of very nice elderly women. Should even a comma be missing, every page of your work was torn up and you were told to retype it. All the other people in this pool were older than me but they were wonderfully kind, and each month when I became ice-cold and racked with period pains, they heaped their coats on me, made me lie on the floor and took over my work. I shall never forget them. I loved them all. Their coats smelt awful, though – of armpits. During coffee breaks, these nice women tried to improve my English: 'Dearie, don't say sofa, say settee. Don't say suit, say costume. Stop saying lavatory, say toilet. You mustn't say sorry, say pardon.'

Every night I scribbled a note to my mother. It was awful that I could not afford the fare to Switzerland to visit her. I worked in London till noon on Saturdays when, by train, bus and walking I reached Stanford Dingley. Our house seemed sad and empty, but with little presents of food and toys, swift visits to see Bob and Kyrle, reading children's story books to my sisters, and bathing in the mill stream, we soon made these happy times. Cynthia and Daphne were always thrilled when I arrived home at the weekends. There was a wonderful fallen-down tree at the top of our garden and every time I returned from London, I would read stories to them on that tree. Returning to London on Sunday evenings was dismal.

Most of my friends and contemporaries were preparing to be presented at Court. For all their frills and feathers, they looked rather silly and I began to feel sorry for the Royals, having to sit while the débutantes of England, stiff with fear, marched by, making rather wobbly curtsies. I could not fathom the point of this exercise: was it possible that this charade could make one socially acceptable? So many young ladies, still encased in puppy fat, looked ridiculous and unhappy, whilst their mothers – dressed to kill – preened themselves and gossiped ceaselessly. I determined not to get involved in this palaver.

Apart from family disasters, life in England in the 1930s was wonderful. Most large houses still had staff, and weekend parties and dances were frequent. More and more young people owned cars and began to explore Europe. The theatre and cinema were extremely good and dance music and lyrics excellent. Sometimes industrial trouble erupted but this seemed to be the responsibility of the old and nothing to do with the young, who hardly noticed it. Most of us now owned a wireless and a camera. Attractive, well-fitting clothes – not expensive – were available in the stores for those who could not afford *haute couture*. White ties and tails and dinner jackets, along with ball, dinner and cocktail dresses were essential. The young were very independent but their reverence for their families was acute. They were courteous and often affectionate to those who served them in town or country.

The immediate future seemed to be a nightmare; our pretty house and garden, and my little sisters would need money, and Nannie Kate wages. My small earnings could not cope

Cynthia, Daphne and me, Ogmore-by-Sea, 1933

(*left*) Owen at RAF Grantham, 1933

(*below*) Kyrle Leng and Bob Gathorn Hardy at Stanford Dingley, 1934

(*above*) Enjoying the sunshine in Spain

(*left*) John Hopton on the beach in Spain

(*above*)
Government
House, Sydney,
Australia, 1937

(*left*) Arriving
in Australia with
the Wakehurst
children on
board the *Orford*

(*above*) Dan Ranfurly, Canberra, Australia

(*below*) Me and Dan, on the left, with our friends at a fancy-dress party in Sydney

Skiing with Elsa Albert, Mount Kosciusko, Australia

(*above*) Our skiing party taking a well-earned break

(*below*) 'Horizontal Herm', the subject of a regular press column!

Our wedding day at St George's Church, Hanover Square,
17 January 1939

with these. If and when my father returned to England, would he have enough money to support us all and his new love? What should I say to family and friends? Though I was now grown up, I found it difficult to remain loyal to everybody, to help everyone and know how to behave. The cost of reaching our mother in Switzerland was insurmountable, and the hope of ever being a happy family again had vanished.

Sometimes good friends took me out to dine and dance; anxious and boring aunts poured useless advice over me; Owen, Nannie Kate and my dog remained my best friends. Food, clothes and small travelling expenses were a constant worry: often lovely invitations had to be refused for lack of a pretty dress or a rail fare. Most of my school friends had rich parents who arranged parties and balls for them and kindly invited me but I had to refuse these because I had not the money to reach them. I

got used to this and so did they, with kind
laughter.

My uncle, Godfrey Llewellyn, short, fat and
very amusing, came to our rescue. He invited
my two little sisters to stay in Wales. I sent all
our furniture to store in my name and locked
up the empty Garden House. I found a job for
Nannie Kate with some cousins, and, with
misery, gave my beloved dog away to a good
home and then retreated to London to work.
It was difficult to forget lovely houses and
gardens. Now Owen, our mother, our father
and my little sisters were out of my reach.

When, to my great sorrow, Grannie Elwes
died, and soon afterwards Grandpapa and
Gran Llewellyn, we children felt lonely. We
had no better friends and their nice houses
had long been sanctuaries to us – of love,
comfort and fun. Now only the Garden House
remained as somewhere to which we really
belonged, but it had become an empty and

unhappy house without our mother and with our heartbroken father behaving like Mr Barratt of Wimpole Street.

To add to my sadness I was stunned to learn that our charming and handsome cousins, David and Francis Llewellyn, our special friends, were dead. Both had started brilliant military careers and were ace shots. Both had always seemed carefree and happy, yet both shot themselves dead. Were these accidents, or on purpose? This mystery was never solved. It reminded me of *Beau Geste*.

Owen seldom got leave. When he did, he always brought his Australian and New Zealand friends with him. 'Their families live very far away,' he used to say, 'so we must shelter them.' They all loved flying and often flew low over our roof and did aerobatics to amuse us.

Owen loved our father and mother but was wiser than me: 'Our mother can't help being ill,' he said, 'but you can't cure her and can only love and comfort her. Our father has been blessed all his life but he has squandered a fortune in record time and must now face the music. You must stop being sad and shattered by their drama and begin to enjoy your own life. Work and play hard and, still loving them, blaze your own trail.' More than anyone else, Owen tried to help me.

As we grew older, embarrassments were frequent. Leaving a very stately home after a lovely weekend, I watched my absent-minded sister, Cynthia, pressing her small tip into the hand of our millionaire host and kissing the butler goodbye. On another occasion, at a ball, a soiled sanitary towel suddenly appeared on the dance floor. At first few noticed it but after a while, as it was shifted around the floor by long, swirling skirts, it became the centre of attention. Our partners steered us carefully round it but, when the music stopped and we all sat down, it remained resplendent on the centre of the dance floor. At last, after what seemed an eternity, a blushing footman carrying a silver salver and sugar tongs removed it, to great applause.

Sometimes, by mistake, we arrived at parties to which we'd not been invited. This was easy to do because dances were going on in London in every direction — often in the same hotel or area. On one dreadful evening when I arrived innocently and cheerfully at the wrong party, a furious host picked me up and flung me out on to the street, ruining my dress and hair-do, and grazing my face. Not long afterwards, when I was married to Dan and we gave a party, he appeared and we had the satisfaction of asking him to leave as he had not been invited.

One morning, very early, before I had

dressed, Aunt Lucy telephoned me. She and
her husband Owlie, Mr Justice Stable, were
great friends of my parents. Though she was
much older than me, Aunt Lucy and I were
tremendous friends and for many years we
shared all our secrets and private thoughts. We
spent much time together: she was a
particularly special woman, who helped me
through disaster and misery. 'I need to see
you urgently,' she said. 'Get a taxi and don't
stop on the way.' She sounded peculiar. When
I arrived, she propelled me into an armchair,
fetched me a cup of coffee and began walking
round and round the room. I wondered if she'd
killed her nice husband or her lazy maid, gone
bankrupt or stolen something. We were
tremendous friends and I knew she'd call on
me if ever she was in trouble. 'What is the
matter?' I asked gently. Suddenly she stopped
walking and turned towards me and I saw she
was crying. 'Your beloved brother, Owen,

has been killed in a mid-air collision,' she said and handed me a newspaper. I read the front page. Both planes had gone down in flames.

I stayed in the armchair for hours unable to move or speak. Now and then I read the newspaper report again, hoping I had read it wrongly the first time. Then I sank back into an abyss of misery and fear.

After she'd had lunch, which I couldn't eat, Aunt Lucy said we could not just sit there and we must do something. She put me in a taxi and we drove to the West End to a matinée. The curtain rose showing a middle-aged couple chatting in a lovely sitting room. Almost at once police arrived and told them that their son had been killed in an air accident. Appalled and speechless, Aunt Lucy dragged me out of my seat and took me back to the spare room in her flat. 'Try to sleep,' she said and gently closed the door.

An avalanche of dreadful questions poured

through my mind. Why had my father not communicated with me? Who should break this terrible news to our mother? What should we tell my little sisters, who hero-worshipped Owen? There would have to be a funeral but Owen's beautiful body could never be in a coffin – there would only be ashes. And how could I survive in our broken family without the love, laughter and wise advice of Owen?

Almost insane with grief and muddled thinking, I longed to escape Aunt Lucy's flat but instinctively I knew she'd been asked to keep me in London. Day turned into night and night into dawn but I could not sleep. At day-break I kissed her goodbye and fled. I telephoned Baglan but got no answer. And from sheer habit I returned on time to my office and found a little comfort from my typewriter, which at least was waiting for me.

I was sure my father would communicate with me, but he didn't. He just sent me a message via Aunt Lucy to say I must not go to Owen's funeral. I was amazed that I was not informed where and when this would be but I did know I should be there. At first I thought that perhaps my father did not want to see my grief – even if I was brave and did not cry – but I could not understand this. I think Owen's death was the end of my father's future.

I thought incessantly of my mother, alone and ill in Switzerland. So recently she'd lost her mother and father, and now her son. I had not enough money to reach her. Day after day, sitting behind a typewriter, I grew sadder and sadder. With our mother marooned in Switzerland, our father absconded, our grandparents and Owen dead, my little sisters lodged with kind but faraway relations, our family had ceased to exist.

I moved into a small flat with Cynthia in Harriet Street, Knightsbridge. It had three nice rooms,

a bathroom and kitchen and cost £3 a week.
We let our spare room to a clever and amusing
cousin who had just had her aquiline nose
operated on to turn it into a snub. She was
hilarious: one cold evening she left for dinner
at the Ritz wearing an evening dress over a
tweed coat and skirt. She looked pregnant but
did not mind.

I had rather a lot of relations, English and
Welsh, and I kept lists of them to help me at
Christmas and Easter, but I dodged their
birthdays. I put them into categories: 'Nice
and fun', 'Bearable', 'Ghastly' and 'Nuts'. I
started another list, but tore it up as it seemed
unkind: it was 'Good looking', 'Plain', and
'Hideous'. Footnotes on all of these were useful
to keep: 'Cheats at cards', 'Nauseating eater',
'Beastly to animals', 'Snob', 'Smells bad',
'Mean', or else, 'Brave', 'Generous',
'Amusing', 'Good rider'.

I always had boyfriends. I generally chose

them according to what kind of car they had! There were two in particular: one was Johnny Hopton, who was tall and attractive and had a marvellous car! His family lived in Cadogan Square in a very grand house.

The other was a heavenly person called Peter Miller Mundy who was incredibly funny. He used to make us all laugh. He owned a turkey which he loved. He put a very light collar and lead round its neck and took it everywhere with him. When he went to stay overnight anywhere it would sit on the end of his bed and start gobbling at dawn and wake the whole house! Peter was fun. His father and mother lived in a lovely house near Salisbury. His mother was mad about music.

Most of us learnt to drive a car by the kindness of the lucky few who owned one. When young officers in the Brigade of Guards were confined to barracks under 'open arrest', they often lent their cars to friends. One

charming but errant acquaintance of mine,
who was continually in trouble, frequently
allowed me to use his swift and beautiful
Lancia. Together with Cynthia and another girl
friend, we shared the cost of oil and petrol,
and gradually explored Europe. Our journeys
took us across the Channel to France, on
through the Black Forest to Munich and thence
to Salzburg, aiming at Hungary.

We all knew French but only a few words
of German. Our favourite word was
'*gr'ad'aus*', which means 'straight on'. We
used it as a game, stopping now and then
to ask people on the road, '*gr'ad'aus?*' Few
ever asked us where we were trying to get to.
They just replied, '*Ja, gr'ad'aus*', and waved
us on.

In the evenings we would stop for the night
at some small inn and dine off Wiener
Schnitzel, Kartoffeln and Kaffee mit Schlag.
Sooner or later a picture of Hitler was shown

in German cinemas and cabarets and the audience would leap to its feet, salute and shout, '*Heil Hitler!*' We never moved, which caused annoyance, and furious officials would arrive to remonstrate. We just sat and said, 'Don't understand', in German until they retreated. We thought Hitler was a great joke and bought coloured picture postcards of him in uniform with the Iron Cross on his chest, and on the back we wrote 'Cross marks place where I slept.' These we posted home. Little did we know what was looming. It never crossed our minds that danger lurked – that anything might change our happy world of peace.

We drove down from the mountains one day and having got to the bottom, to where we were staying in a little pub, an enormously tall, red-haired man got off our spare wheel. We didn't know he was there. He said, 'Thanks for the lift.' It was Peter Miller Mundy; he

had been hanging on to our rear wheel all the
way down the Austrian Alps! He had wrapped
himself around it and got a lift away from his
mother who had wanted him at the opera. He
attached himself to us, so when we returned
to England he came too. His mother then
asked us to go and stay with them at their grand
house near Salisbury. I think that of all my
friends Peter made me laugh more than
anybody.

Weeks passed. I stayed in London, working
and seeing my friends. Cynthia was with me
most of the time. I was very fond of her and
took much care of her but she was marvellously
slow at everything. One day she stopped in the
middle of Piccadilly to do up her shoe lace,
and she ate so slowly that when you had got to
your pudding, she would be starting her *hors
d'oeuvres*. Nannie Kate sent me a postcard from
America, where she had gone on her new job.
She wrote, 'I do not like America, the food

or chewing gum. Shall return to civilization shortly.'

For the first time, I went to a cocktail party. Most of the people there were very well dressed and older than me. A few of them talked to me. A waiter carried round a tray of different coloured cocktails. He told me their names: White Lady, Martini, Bacardi, etc. I chose a different colour each time he passed me, to see which I liked best. After I'd tried several, he became less friendly and seemed to avoid me. When people began to leave I set off on foot to dine with Aunt Lucy. I felt happy and sang most of the way. She gave me her usual wonderful welcome and then took me to her bathroom to wash my hands before dinner. Almost at once it seemed as if her wash-basin and loo were doing a tango so I sat down on the floor and watched. Quite soon they made me dizzy and sick. When Aunt Lucy came to see why I had been so long, I explained to her that she must call a plumber because her bathroom equipment had broken loose and was whizzing about. She removed me to her spare bedroom and put me to bed. Before she closed the door she asked where I had been. Knowing she was old-fashioned, I tried to explain: 'To something called a cocktail party which has nothing to do with poultry but where you stand up and drink revolting liquids with rather revolting people.' She switched off the light and gently closed the door.

After a considerable time my father telephoned me. He'd returned to England and found the Garden House empty and locked up. He was furious but not nearly as angry as me. He demanded his furniture. He said he'd put the Garden House up for sale and bought a house on Dartmoor called Prince Hall and urgently needed his furniture. Determined not to be rude or risk a quarrel, I said very little except to remind him he still had three children and that until he provided somewhere for us to live, I would release no furniture.

Many days later he came to see me in London. He told me he was going to Switzerland to ask our mother for a divorce so that he could marry again. Though for days I'd felt furious with him, the sight of him filled me with pity. He looked small and desperate – like a child who had got into a gigantic muddle. It was typical of our mother that she helped him: 'Poor Griff,' she wrote later to me. 'I must release him to have a less lonely life.' And without resentment, she divorced him.

Gradually I realized it might be best for my father to remarry. Over and over again he'd tried to help my mother fight her terrible illness and over and over again her illness had overwhelmed us all. He was dreadfully sad and desperately lonely. Obviously he still adored her but her deep depressions and ferocious periods when she stormed at everyone had become increasingly difficult for him.

After some months working at the War Office typing pool, Miss Roads sent for me. She explained that because so many officers of the regular army were being retired a new office was being opened in Pall Mall to help them find civilian jobs. Four senior generals would run this office. 'Hundreds of officers need work and wages to augment their pensions,' she said and added: 'This is not just a job – it's a crusade.' I thanked her and promised to do my level best. I agreed to start work next morning. My hours were 10 a.m. till 4 p.m., my wage £4 a week. I was happy working for the four old generals from the First World War and it was exciting when we found good jobs for retired regular army officers who so urgently needed work and wages. We had a nice office close by Green

Park and were kept busy, as, sadly, so many needed help.

I had worked for them for quite a time, when one day a boring and bossy female acquaintance telephoned me and said in her shrill, superior voice, 'I've just the job for you and have made an appointment for you to be interviewed.' She rang off before I could tell her to mind her own business. I was perfectly happy with my old generals; I loved working for them. Not wanting to be rude to anyone, I consulted them and they insisted I keep the appointment.

I arrived in Lennox Gardens to see a Lord and Lady Wakehurst. He was very tall with a rather red, fleshy face and she looked severe — perhaps because she wore no make-up. Quickly I explained I was not looking for a job, that there had been a misunderstanding. They did not appear to listen and, after a few questions, said I was just what they were looking for and asked if I could be ready to sail for Australia in two weeks' time. Astonished and embarrassed, I asked if I might have one day to think it over. Then I thanked them for their offer and fled. Lord Wakehurst was Governor Designate for New South Wales.

The old generals and my family all said this was an opportunity not to be missed – it was a great chance to see the world. After a lot of dithering, I called up Miss Roads at the War Office and arranged my replacement for the generals and then accepted the Wakehursts' offer. I said I'd go for one year and be ready in a fortnight. I felt sick with fear lest this be a big mistake.

1937

Two weeks later, I found myself at Tilbury docks where a little crowd of Wakehurst family and staff were waiting to embark on a liner called *Orford*: three small boys, a nannie, a comptroller, two ADCs, two cooks, two footmen and a lady's maid. After endless farewells we sailed and I took refuge in my cabin, dismayed by the look of them all and appalled at what I'd done to myself. Before long the Bay of Biscay convinced me I was about to drown and I began to think this might be a good idea.

Sun and the Mediterranean, where we called at several ports and went ashore, helped a little but, except for Lady Wakehurst, I found the party rather difficult to like: the children were very spoilt; Lord Wakehurst very silent; one aide very grand and the other very dim; and worst of all the lady's maid was odious and was terribly rude to Lady Wakehurst: 'Will you wear your hideous pink or your hideous blue today, Your Ladyship?' she'd say. The captain and crew of the *Orford* were charming and kind.

I survived fairly well until one day when I wore trousers, which horrified the Wakehurst family and I was asked to remove them.

It took five weeks to reach Australia. At Fremantle, in spite of a kind welcome, we were all rather stunned by its bleak appearance. But we cheered up at Melbourne, where we had a delicious and amusing lunch with Lord Huntingfield at Government House. Our arrival at Sydney was grand and comic. Outside the harbour, Lord and Lady Wakehurst were transferred to a battleship. Then the *Orford* steamed into the magnificent harbour and deposited the rest of us on the docks where, with the two eldest boys, I was hurried off by car to nearby Government House and taken to sit in the gallery of the ballroom so we could watch the swearing-in ceremony. When Lord Wakehurst, dressed in full Governor's regalia, arrived in the ballroom and was seated on a kind of throne, the little boys burst into peals of shrill laughter and I almost had to smother them with my fur stole to silence them.

After lunch, when formalities ended, Lady Wakehurst and I explored Government House to allocate rooms for guests, nurseries and staff. On the edge of Sydney Harbour, with gardens running down almost to the water, this Victorian building had a superb view and pleasant rooms up and downstairs, but the furniture was hideous and uncomfortable: china jugs, basins and chamber-pots adorned all the bedrooms, and buttoned sofas and armchairs made all downstairs rooms painful to the eye and the behind. We decided that when we had the time and money we'd have fun making the house prettier and more comfortable. Next morning we learned this might not be easy because there were only two large stores in Sydney.

At first we must have seemed stuffy and pompous to the Australians, because we were all on our best behaviour. This did not last long. Lord Wakehurst, who had no small talk, soon became known as 'The Two Minutes Silence' because, after dinner parties when each lady guest was taken to sit next to him, he never said anything and prayed the lady would chatter. Lady Wakehurst, whenever she had to make a speech, shook from head to foot with terror and made me hold her hand to steady her. People soon recognized how kind and charming both Wakehursts were and quickly they became very popular. Their staff, including me, received marvellous hospitality and our frequent mistakes were welcomed with hilarity.

Soon after our arrival our handsome senior ADC, Tony Lawrence, began spitting blood. I told Lady Wakehurst and to our horror it was found he had cancer of the lung. He had to be flown home to die and we were devastated.

The Governor General of Australia was Lord

Gowrie, whose main house was in Canberra. He also had a nice house in Sydney on the edge of the harbour. His staff became our great friends and allies – Dan Ranfurly and Tony Llewellyn-Palmer. Both were mobbed by beautiful Australian girls.

After a short time in Sydney it became necessary for the Wakehursts to tour around New South Wales and get to know its peoples. Mundy, the lady's maid, refused to accompany them and so I was taken instead to wash and iron their clothes, type letters and look after them. At first we travelled by train but at the end of the line we went in a convoy of cars. Their Excellencies, with a motor-cycle escort, bowled along ahead, but we who followed travelled in a cloud of suffocating dust. On one occasion I was so dirty Lady Wakehurst mistook me for an Aboriginal.

We travelled enormous distances and stayed on many grand stations whose owners had thousands of livestock and acres of grazing land. Their hospitality and food were superb but their plumbing was surprising. Nearly all their lavatories were earthen closets and some of these were five seaters. I never dared ask if they all sat down together. As far as we were concerned, the Wakehursts went first and staff followed in order of age. Being the youngest, I had to go last and pray the convoy would not leave without me. Poor Kenneth Harding, their senior staff, found this unbearable and three weeks after we left Sydney, he confided in me that he had not 'been' since then.

Our furthest stop was Tipoburra, where I was persuaded to ride in a camel race. I was hoisted on to an unfriendly animal called Dot. I came in second but had difficulty in dismounting, as she was keen to bite anything in front of her and had diarrhoea all over her behind.

We returned to Sydney exhausted but filled

with admiration for the country we had seen
and the people we had met. It was nice to have
hot baths again and to get mail from home.

One day, back at Government House, my
beloved and beautiful parrot – given to me by
Sydney's zoo – flew off my shoulder to the top
of a high pine tree. Making loving noises, I
climbed after it but just when I had nearly
reached it, it flew off into the public park. Still
uttering endearments, I climbed the iron spiked
fence which divided Government House
garden from the public park but unfortunately
I slipped and an iron spike pierced the palm
of my right hand and cut an artery. Getting it
off the spike was ghastly. Luckily an aide saw
what had happened and rushed a car into the
park to carry me to hospital. It was announced
that my right hand must be cut off because it
was so coated with pitch pine. A charming
and distinguished surgeon arrived. I beseeched
him not to cut off my hand but sew it up.

Luckily I made him laugh, so he said he'd try to clean and stitch it up. 'It'll be hell for you,' he said, 'but it's worth a try.' Hours of agony ensued but somehow he dug out the pitch pine and stitched up the awful hole in the palm of my hand. We became great friends.

Soon after I emerged from hospital we all went to stay with the Gowries at Government House, Canberra. One fine morning, when there was no work to do, Dan Ranfurly took me for a ride. My right arm was in a sling. All went well until we turned to go home, when Lady Gowrie's unattractive pony, which I was riding, bolted on a wide stretch of grass about a mile from Government House. It had a mouth of iron and I could not pull it up with my left hand. Soon it trod in a hole at speed and turned turtle and I hit the ground very hard but, miraculously, my arm stayed in its sling and, apart from a bloody nose, I was none the worse.

In those days Sydney had only one major hotel and two main stores. But the population was very well dressed and their houses, mainly flanking the harbour, were well furnished. Many people owned beautiful boats. There was one nightclub which all the young frequented. This was difficult for me to reach because once the Governor returned home in the evenings the tall iron gates to Government House were locked. As we all wore long evening dresses, I found it difficult to climb over these and often got hooked up and had to ask our sentries to rescue me.

We had two splendid Australian ADCs, who were wonderfully kind to us. After a while one of them, Alexis Albert, and his charming wife asked the Wakehursts if they could take me to ski on Mount Kosciusko for ten days. We drove from Sydney to the base hotel and thence in a horse-drawn cab as far as snow would allow. Then we had to 'herring-bone' all the way to the ski hotel, a building divided in two, one half for men and the other for women. It was primitive, with just dormitories; we lived rough but it was fun and funny. A dog team was kept to pull a sleigh to the summit of Mount Kosciusko. Press were everywhere and soon they began writing a column called 'Horizontal Herm', which was about me because they seldom saw me standing upright.

The year we were in Australia was the sesquicentenary of the discovery of New South Wales and huge celebrations were arranged. The British government sent its Lord Privy Seal to represent it, and all state Governors and the Governors General of Australia and New Zealand, along with their aides, arrived to stay with us. Several British warships anchored in our harbour. Banquets, parades and balls took place and nearly every night magnificent fireworks lit up the skies.

Two things amused the ADCs and me: one of the state Governors had a dreadful affliction which caused him to frequently and suddenly belch for several minutes on end, no matter where he was or when. He'd go off like a machine gun causing astonishment and appalling struggles not to laugh, especially in banquets, church services and receptions. The other was the Lord Privy Seal, who we'd expected would be a distinguished elderly man. On his first night at Government House, he woke and terrified me by plunging, naked, through my mosquito net. Only by threatening to scream did I manage to make him retreat to his own room. Not deterred by finding me a dud, he pursued many of Sydney's attractive girls. He had a fixed routine: a small bunch of flowers prior to an invitation to dine, then a brief dance in a nightclub, followed by an onslaught in a taxi and then, hopefully, a skirmish to bed. Poor Lord and Lady

Wakehurst became anxious about his adventures. Mr David Lloyd-Jones, owner of Sydney's top store and a good friend, kindly sent us a beautiful blonde mannequin from his shop window. We placed this in the Lord Privy Seal's bed, but sadly it was found each morning seated on a lavatory. Finally, when the Lord Privy Seal was seen in a nightclub clutching a pair of knickers from which its owner had only just escaped, Lord Wakehurst read the riot act to our distinguished visitor and for a while peace reigned.

Soon after these celebrations, Dan Ranfurly, whose term of work for the Governor General was over, departed for England. I felt dreadfully sad, and also afraid. He was so attractive I felt he might well find someone better than me in Hollywood, New York or in the London Season. We'd become great friends. He was tall, elegant and charming and I knew I could never love anyone so much.

Towards the end of my promised year with the Wakehursts, my friend in Sydney's travel office informed me that someone had died on a world cruise ship and his cabin was available at a cut price. The ship would call at Sydney soon and sail on via New Zealand, Fiji, Honolulu, America and Panama to England. Gratefully I handed over my savings, which were just enough, to grab this offer.

Luckily my replacement for the Wakehursts had just arrived so that I was able to hand over my work carefully before sailing away. It was dreadfully sad to say goodbye to the Wakehursts and many Australian friends but I was longing to see my family and England again and, above all, Dan Ranfurly.

SS *Franconia* was a nice ship with a superb English crew who coped brilliantly with a rather surprising load of passengers. They told me to keep my cabin door locked. It emerged that many people sent their old or dotty relations on world cruises so as to give themselves a rest. Some charming elderly American women told me, with much laughter, which passengers were sane or not.

On my first morning I watched an elderly American man, who talked loudly to himself, throwing deck chairs into the sea. No one took any notice. Soon afterwards a ghastly little man wandered up to me and said: 'I'm taking you with me to Alaska. You are just what I've been looking for.' Luckily an old woman came and sat down next to me and he departed. Coated in jewellery and wearing a tiara, she said, 'You should wear more jewellery or people will think you are common. But maybe you are common. Then only God can help you.' Soon she too wandered off.

There were many nice and amusing passengers to talk to but I did enjoy the eccentrics and especially an enormous elderly woman who appeared from time to time on the top deck wearing only a lace bra and frilly transparent knickers. She performed hideous little dances and, rather touchingly, occasionally waited for applause. Her bosoms frequently escaped her poor little bra.

The *Franconia* called at Fiji and Honolulu for passengers to look around. Before we reached Los Angeles I learnt that if I got off there – instead of going through the Panama Canal – I would get a good rebate and so, on reaching America, I left the ship and paid $35 to travel by Greyhound bus to New York via Salt Lake City, Omaha, Chicago and Washington.

The bus stopped every two hours for a ten-minute 'comfort pause' and soon I learned to wash at the first stop, eat at the second and take a little walk at the third. I got off for one night in Chicago – a little apprehensive of gangsters – and another in Washington, where I saw the White House. In New York, armed with the keys of the apartment of some kind

old ladies on the *Franconia*, I was collected
by Monty Moore Montgomery, who took
me all over the city and to dine and dance.
When the *Franconia* docked in New York,
I returned to my cabin and set sail for
England.

The day after I got home, when I returned
to our flat from shopping, I found Dan
Ranfurly seated on my sofa, reading the *Sporting
Life*. Seldom had I been so surprised or pleased.
I'd worried lest he might have forgotten me,
as he'd journeyed home via Hollywood and
New York and must have met so many
fascinating girls. Also I'd forgotten to give him
my address in London and I had no idea of
where to contact him in England. 'How on
earth did you find me?' I asked. 'I've kept track
of you for months – right across the world,'
he said. 'But that's no fun. Why don't we just
get married?'

Dan had bought a big blue four-seater Buick

when he was in America. It went very fast. When I got back to England he was zooming around in it everywhere! Whenever we went out in it we always sat in one seat together – we were inseparable.

1938

As soon as I got back to England from Australia it was vital I find a job because I had almost no money left. Furthermore my sister, Cynthia, previously so loving, instantly made it clear that I was not welcome in our flat in Harriet Street. 'I've had more fun with you out of the way,' she announced in her amusing candid manner. 'You can sleep on the divan in the sitting-room but you must keep your clothes in your suitcase and have only third call on the bathroom.'

Someone told me that a Miss Dorothy Paget

needed a secretary. I knew nothing about her except that she owned racehorses. I wrote and asked for an interview and got a swift reply to go at once to see her. The next day at noon, clad in my best apple-green overcoat, I rang the bell at 8 Balfour Place, Mayfair, as instructed. A smiling butler opened the door and led me into a nice ground-floor sitting-room where I was welcomed by three charming elderly women who all seemed to be Russian. Madame Orloff, Madame Dykelli and Madame Fregosi. 'Dorothy,' they said, 'is fast asleep and won't wake up for hours, or perhaps until tomorrow, so you must stay and lunch with us and wait just in case she wakes and wants to see you.' They told me that my hours would be from 12 noon to 12 midnight, my pay £12 a week. But that I must shed my green overcoat 'as Dorothy thinks green is unlucky'. After a superb lunch and dinner, just on midnight I was allowed to go home. I went to

Dan's flat to tell him I was to return to Balfour Place at noon the next day.

Miss Paget was still asleep when I arrived at Balfour Place next morning, clad in my second-best coat. After another delicious lunch everything became electric. The butler announced Miss Paget was awake and was leaving immediately for Sandown racecourse and we were all to go too. Madame Orloff said that Dorothy was very shy and would want to look at me through field glasses before she might consider taking me on. She added, 'Miss Paget has a runner today at Sandown. Thank heaven you are not wearing your green coat.'

Two expensive cars purred outside the front door. I was put in the second car with the Russians and, quite suddenly, an enormous female hurtled out of the house, climbed into the driver's seat of the front car and sped off at surprising speed. We had difficulty in keeping up.

At the races Miss Paget kept her distance from the Russians and me. In a dilapidated tweed coat she watched her horse run unsuccessfully and after a quick talk with her trainer she sped off for home, taking Madame Orloff with her. Regardless of traffic signs, very fast and brilliantly, she reached her front door, shot out of her car, left the engine running, dashed to the lift and vanished upstairs.

'You have the job,' said Madame Orloff. 'She liked the look of you. But you can't go home yet in case she wishes to speak to you.' After a delicious dinner and more waiting, but with no sign of Miss Paget, at midnight I was driven home in another lovely car.

Next day at noon I began to work for Miss Paget, with Madame Fregosi, typing letters and documents in a nice little office just inside the front door. There was no sign of Miss Paget but the Russians gave me an affectionate welcome and an excellent lunch. They referred to me as 'the child'. They talked sadly of Russia, and said that Dorothy was doing wonderful things for Russian refugees. They told me that she slept a lot and ate a lot, that she kept no normal hours, so they must be awake and alert day and night lest she need them. They managed to get enough sleep by taking turns to be on duty. These three ladies had escaped from Russia with their lives but little else. Their kindness and wonderful manners amazed me. They never grumbled and always spoke loyally of Miss Paget.

Perhaps because I'd known sadness in my own family it did not take me long to realize that Dorothy Paget was a dreadful tragedy. She was clever, quite young, immensely rich, and marvellously generous to those she recognized as unfortunate – particularly aristocratic refugees from Russia. But she was abnormally shy and hid herself day and night from the world she belonged to. Sometimes humble, often arrogant, she would stay awake for several days and nights on end and then go to sleep, perhaps for several days and nights. In between waking and sleeping she ate enormous meals of luxury food which were kept ready round the clock so as to be instantly available should she demand them.

Whether she had grown so gross and ugly from over-eating I could not tell but when I first saw her close to I was stunned by her size and ugliness. She looked bloated and about to burst. Nevertheless her household – the Russians, her butler, chef, chauffeurs and maids – all seemed to like and respect her, although they were a little afraid of her because she always demanded instant service of every kind by day and night. She had only one visitor – a young woman who I think was a cousin who came often and stayed for hours.

After nearly two months, Miss Paget suddenly asked to see me. Up in the lift I went and found her in bed in a huge room. A big table laden with marvellous food was wheeled in just behind me. Stupidly I said, 'Oh, Miss Paget, if you have a lunch party, I mustn't stay long.' 'Guests?' she said sharply. 'Certainly not. That's my lunch.' After an awkward silence she said, 'I want to know if you have a boyfriend.' I told her I was engaged to Dan Ranfurly. She was horrified. She said her Russians loved me, my work was excellent, and this was a catastrophe. 'Go away, go away,' she said. 'This is dreadful news and I must think.' I turned at the door and was stunned to see she was crying.

Young, intelligent, very rich, but bloated with food so that her face was revolting and her body enormous, she had made herself into a monster. Her Russian refugees, her horses and her food were her only interests. By nature shy, her appearance had made her want to hide. Now she was a recluse. After lunch I sent her a little note: 'Be sure that after I'm married I would still love to come often and see you all.'

When I gave notice of leaving, soon before my wedding, there were dreadful upsets. Day after day the Russians explained it would make Dorothy sad, perhaps ill, though I had hardly ever seen her. And they wept. I had grown fond of them all and hated to see them cry. But one day I forced myself to leave and after I'd hugged them goodbye, Dan drove me away in his car to escape. I felt as if I'd deserted the Russians but also that I'd escaped from a prison. I asked Dorothy and all of them to our wedding – but only the butler came.

One of the nice things about the wedding was that I asked one child from every family who had helped me through the terrible years of my unhappy childhood to be a bridesmaid.

There was a child connected with every part of my life at my wedding. By doing this I tried to repay a debt to each person who had helped me. I also had an Elwes page and a Llewellyn page – I tried to organize it so that nobody was forgotten. Cynthia was very jealous of me all the time so she didn't really help me with the wedding. I went out and bought the most superb length of white brocade – it was really rather beautiful. Our family dressmaker was cheap and made square-length sleeves and a little high-waisted dress in this marvellous material.

Dan's family was very nice to me but rather worried that a penniless girl with a difficult family was marrying into their family. I learnt a lot about snobbery. The Ranfurlys were very poor too.

1939

On 17 January 1939 I woke early to suddenly
remember it was my wedding day. I
telephoned my mother in Switzerland to tell
her how sad I felt that she could not be with
Dan and me on our happiest day and promised
we'd visit her soon after our honeymoon.

I donned my nice white brocade dress and
our family veil, which had been worn on better
heads than mine over many years, and then my
twelve little bridesmaids and pages arrived in
their white satin dresses and suits. My father
collected me and I felt nervous as we drove
to St George's Church in Hanover Square until
I saw Dan waiting for me, and then I became
encased in happiness and oblivious of anyone
else. There was an amazing parson at St
George's. I remembered when I was nearly at

the altar that I hadn't taken the price off the soles of my shoes and they had cost me something like twenty-nine and six! At the reception afterwards, I gave a little present to each of my small attendants and tried to thank many of the guests for the help they had given me over the years.

After the reception there was a farewell and Dan and I got in the car to make our way to the airport and Dan's mother, Hilda, jumped in the car with us to come to the airport too! But just the two of us flew away on our honeymoon.

We spent a night at the Ritz in Paris and then sped off to Cortina d'Ampezzo in Italy to ski. Dan hired a delightful guide, Zardini, to lead us down the various steep and fascinating runs. One day, at lunch-time, when many people assembled at a chalet to eat, we noticed a very beautiful woman, a superb skier, with her boyfriend. She had a dreadful scar from ear to ear and across her nose. Zardini told us this was not unusual. 'You see,' he said, 'she has been unfaithful and so has been held down and sliced from ear to ear and across her nose as a punishment. This is quite normal.' Dan and I were appalled.

We skied all and every day and after a bath and dinner we danced. No one and nothing seemed to exist for me but Dan. We were supremely happy – just the two of us.

After our honeymoon we moved into Dan's little flat in Clarges Street. He had bought another single bed but we only used one. Little did we realize that the Second World War was about to begin.